advance praise for
QUEENS OF NOISE

"Beautiful prose, spot-on colourful, descriptive characters packed into an electric, lively novella. I really loved the community and relationship between the characters. I fell hard for the crush between Mixi and R."
—Tlotlo Tsamaase, author of *The Silence of the Wilting Skin*

"Gorgeous with grit. A yip-yowling punk adventure with funny moments and feeling moments that gush together into a story as rich as your bloodstream."
—Meg Elison, author of *The Book of the Unnamed Midwife*

"Leigh Harlen's *Queens of Noise* is a queer punk power anthem; it sings, it stomps, it pushes you into a bathroom stall and kisses you with tongue (but only with your explicit consent). It's a queercore dirtbag ballad with sharp teeth and a soft heart."
—Nino Cipri, author of *FINNA*

"...readers will appreciate the sensitive, nuanced treatment of the LGBTQ pack members and the moments of humor. Anarchic, bighearted, and fun, this scruffy tale will appeal to fans of urban fantasy and queer paranormal romance..."
—*Publishers Weekly*

Neon Hemlock Press
www.neonhemlock.com
@neonhemlock

Queens of Noise
Leigh Harlen

This novella is entirely a work of fiction. Names,
characters, places and incidents are the products of
the author's imagination or are used fictitiously. Any
resemblance to actual events, locales, organizations or
persons, living or dead, is entirely coincidental.

Cover Illustration by Crystal Araiza
Cover Design by dave ring

ISBN-13: 978-1-952086-01-4

Leigh Harlen
QUEENS OF NOISE

Neon Hemlock Press

THE 2020 NEON HEMLOCK NOVELLA SERIES

Queens of Noise

BY LEIGH HARLEN

For all those who went out into the world to find their families.

and

For Alison, who is forever and always the heart of my own family.

CHAPTER 1

Sometimes you have to show a little fang. I try not to do it. But, once in a while, my tough aesthetic and take-no-shit attitude isn't enough to deter the truly awful and the awfully helpful. The trouble is, norms will tolerate shifters, so long as we behave ourselves. But the second we indicate that we'll bite back if someone pushes us hard enough, then they run through the streets screaming about monsters. I learned that real quick when they ran me and my pack out of Felton, calling us queers and werewolves. The queer part was right, though not sure why it was such a problem, but we were werecoyotes, not wolves. As if I could ever be one of those uptight, bougie assholes.

"Where you headed, young lady? I'll give you a lift." He had gray hair cut short, probably trying to minimize the fact it was rapidly receding, as if getting old was something to be feared instead of envied. Judging by the shitty tie covered in cartoons he was definitely somebody's dad; maybe even somebody's granddad.

"Nah. I'm good. Thanks though."

He didn't leave. He and his rust-bucket car kept creeping along beside me, window down. "Come on, get in the car. It's late and a little thing like you oughtn't be out alone."

I turned towards him and shifted my face. The moon would

be full tomorrow night so it was easy. Nose and mouth extended almost, but not quite into a snout, and sharp teeth pierced through my gums, pushing the dull, human teeth to the back.

"Hey mister. Who says she's alone?" Otter-Pup said, unseen. His voice poured from the bushes behind me, thin, high, and ghost-like.

The creep's eyes widened and he slammed his foot down on the gas pedal so hard that the engine screamed in protest. His tires left the stink of burning rubber in the air as he roared away.

Otter-Pup hopped out of the bushes, laughing. He was a dizzying palette of colors from his electric blue hair to his glittery purple suit to the thick rainbow of eyeshadow on his light brown eyelids. I draped my arm over his shoulders, the metal studs of his jacket snagging on the black mesh of my sleeves. That was cool, mesh looked better with some tears in it.

"Where's the rest of the pack?"

He squirmed out from under my arm to sculpt his spiked hair. "They wanted to grab drinks before the show. They're going to meet us at The Mechanical Anatomy." Seeing my face tense, he added, "They took all our gear with them."

I was not happy they'd left Otter-Pup to travel on his own, especially after the asshole I ran into, but he was an adult now. Barely. He could have gone with them or spoken up if he didn't want to walk to the show alone.

We traveled in companionable silence, excitement and nervousness sparking between us, until we arrived at The Mechanical Anatomy. The mildewed entrance had been literally carved into the remains of a staircase. The jumble of jagged, busted stairs was covered by a rickety wooden ramp. At the bottom was a bouncer in a torn t-shirt under a black leather. He crossed his massive, tattooed arms over his chest.

"Hey, Mixi. Otter. Y'all playing tonight?" he asked.

"We are," I said.

"Hell of a line up." He stepped aside and let us through the entryway.

Inside, the floor was sticky with old booze and the air smelled like sweat, cigarettes, and hairspray. The studded, tattooed, mostly black-clad crowd bounced and writhed with abandon to the sound of a band I had never heard before. They didn't smell like shifters, but there was a hint of magic. Witches, maybe. The screen behind them said "Baba Yaga and the Tricky Bitches" in red letters that looked like they'd been carved into skin with a knife. They were pretty good, especially the lead singer. Every bit of her visible skin was covered in tattoos of animals in different art styles. Some were stick 'n poke, others American Traditional, a couple Japanese-style, and one hyper realistic chicken spread across her chest. I was bad at judging how old someone was, but she was young. Fuck, all the bands seemed young to me now. Thirty-three was practically dead in punk years.

Gemini slipped through the crowd towards us, their eyes wide with a look that said, "Un-fucking-believable." We'd been a band together long before the whole werecoyote thing happened and they were the closest to my age, with black skin and an electric pink mohawk. They were a huge nerd. Tonight, they were dressed like a punk rock Sherlock Holmes with a ripped plaid jacket that hung down to their calves and decorated with spikes, buttons, and patches.

They grabbed my arm and leaned in, their whiskey and menthol breath tickled my nose. "R and the wolves are here."

"Shit. Are they playing?"

They nodded vigorously.

"Well, toss back a shot because we're going to have to kick some ass tonight," I said.

Gemini grinned, a hint of fang popping through their gums.

"I know the full moon is coming, but keep it in check. We're here to play, not pick a fight."

"Yeah, yeah. I got you Mama C."

I glared at them. I wasn't sure when the nickname Mama C started. But at my protests that I was nobody's Mama, it turned into Mx. C which became Mixi. Only Gemini still got away with calling me Mama C, usually when I was being protective or bossy.

"Where's everybody else?" Otter-Pup asked.

"Keeping an eye on our gear. Just in case the wolves try something."

"Good call," I said.

We fought our way to the bar. "Double shot of tequila for me, whatever beer is the cheapest mixed with cider for him, and a whiskey shot for them." I pointed at Otter-Pup and Gemini respectively.

The bartender poured and handed the drinks to us. "Ten bucks," she said.

"We're with Mangy Rats," I said.

"Four bucks. That one already drank their comped drinks."

I glared at Gemini who smiled and shrugged. "This is coming out of your cut if we win," I said.

"Fair enough."

We took our drinks and squeezed through the dancing crowd to the doors in the back. When the door clicked shut behind us, the music was muffled to a dull pulse. The air was damp, the floor concrete, and uncovered pipes ran along the ceiling and dripped what I hoped was water on the floor.

Juniper and Rowan sat pressed against one another. Juniper's curly, natural red mohawk flowed all the way down to her lower back and had bits of paint stuck to it from the peeling wall behind her. Her pale cheeks flushed peach; she and Rowan had clearly been making out. Probably the reason they'd wanted to leave early. Otter-Pup was perceptive enough to stay home. Gemini, on the other hand, was not, and had probably spent the last hour as their unwitting third wheel. It was funny. I wasn't sure why they didn't just say they were fucking. No one cared.

"Dead and Disorderly is playing," I said.

Rowan wrinkled his nose. "Why? Battle of the Bands is always punk. Goth posers have Dracula's Ball in October."

I chuckled. "I guess they didn't get the memo. But, I'm for sure not gonna let R upstage us on our own turf. So, everybody get warmed up because we have to kill it out there tonight. Metaphorically." I glanced at Gemini, who nipped the air playfully.

They all began to prepare in their own ways, Otter-Pup by checking over his collection of numerous, quirky instruments. An airhorn, a harmonica, strips of sheet metal, and god only knew what else he'd collected. Gemini jumped up and down, tapping the air with their drumsticks. Rowan and Juniper fingered their guitars while I tended to my vocals, running warm ups and downing shots of tequila.

When at last we were called to the stage, we grabbed our instruments and stepped out under the bright lights. I made eye contact with each member of the band and was pleased they all looked determined, excited, and only a little scared shitless. Gemini grinned and gave me a thumbs up.

"Let's blow their fucking heads off." Juniper grinned and struck a power pose with her guitar.

The crowd clapped and screamed. We only had ten minutes. We had to make it count.

Gemini counted us off and we roared to life with one of our most popular songs, "Shit Gets Bitter." I loved to play it because it showcased what a brilliant weirdo Otter-Pup was and he got to play every single one of his instrument collection. While I growled and shrieked about growing up queer in a world that hated us, he banged and flapped his sheet metal, smashed a sealed bag of old chipped glasses with a hammer, and even buzzed on a kazoo. The crowd fucking loved it. They stomped and cheered and someone threw their underwear at him. We slid into a new track, "Life's Not Easy (But I Am)," that put me and Juniper center stage. She thrashed and slammed the strings of her guitar while I jumped and danced, growling the words menacingly and crescendoing to a raw scream. Then we slipped back into "Shit Gets Bitter" and closed on a crash of drums and squeal of guitar.

The audience thundered and stamped their feet. Otter-Pup grinned over at me. We absolutely murdered our set, no way were we not going to the final three. I waved and touched hands with a group of girls in the front row who screamed, "I love you, Mixi!" then we hustled off the stage for the next band.

Backstage, I grabbed an old towel from my bag and wiped my face, still running high from our killer performance. Rowan and Juniper disappeared into the bathroom, probably to screw. Gemini went out to the bar to flirt for drinks while Otter-Pup and I watched the rest of the bands.

The next two bands were good, but not great. Then came Dead and Disorderly. R Chakrabarti glided across the stage on strappy black shoes, the heel styled to look like a literal stiletto, her hips rolling with wolfish grace. The light dimmed to a smoky silver, giving her warm umber skin a deathly pallor. R's lush, wavy black hair long was streaked with cobalt that perfectly matched her lipstick. The left side of her head was shaved, a Luna moth tattooed on the side as if perched on her ear. She stepped up to the microphone, and the room went silent. It wasn't just her; the entire band was pretty. Stunning, if I was being honest. Huge, sleek, and menacing as if they embodied their wolf alter-egos. Their clothes were a mix of tight and flowing, leather and lace, but all black.

They began to play. Soft chimes, synthesizers that hissed and popped like the band had found them after sitting for thirty-years in a dusty basement, and the gentle whine of an electric violin. R's voice was powerful and exquisite, low and menacing. When she sang, I could feel myself transported to a beautiful garden full of flowers and death.

They went into a fast, raucous number about a woman on a murder spree that let the guitars and R's gleeful, threatening voice shine. When they finished the crowd screamed their approval. When I glanced at Otter-Pup he was watching me and smirking. "What?"

He shrugged and his smirk deepened. "Nothing. They were good, huh?"

"I guess." I crossed my arms. "For frilly goth crap."

The members of Dead and Disorderly waved, R blew kisses, and they left the stage. When the crowd settled down, Lala, the owner of Mechanical Anatomy, came onto the stage.

"That was one hell of a show tonight. But, only three bands can make it to the Battle of the Bands final showdown for a chance to win $1000 and ten hours of free studio time, courtesy of the badass folks at Studio Scream." She paused to allow the crowd to clap politely. "After a very scientific calculation of how hard y'all cheered, I got the names right here." The crowd chuckled as she pulled an envelope from her pocket.

Otter-Pup grabbed my hand tight.

"Who wants to know which bands made it to the showdown?"

Lala crowed.

The crowd clapped and hooted.

"I don't think y'all are excited enough. I said, who wants to know which bands made it to the showdown?"

The crowd shouted, whooped, and stomped louder.

"That's more like it. Alright. First, we got: Baba Yaga and the Tricky Bitches."

Everyone cheered and clapped. A handful of groupies and band loyalists booed.

"Dead and Disorderly."

R and her pack shouted and hugged one another. Otter-Pup's grip on my hand tightened and my heart raced. We had to make it to the showdown. We needed that money and we had kicked ass up there. We deserved this.

"And finally, Mangy Rats! Congratulations and good luck, y'all." Lala jumped off the stage and made her way through the crowd. Everyone began to bob and dance as music blasted over the speakers.

"Holy shit, we did it." I scooped Otter-Pup up in a hug. He laughed and kissed me on both cheeks. Gemini, Juniper, and Rowan forced their way through the crowd to us and we cheered and hugged in jubilation.

"Shit, Dead and Disorderly is gonna be hard to beat," Gemini said.

"We can do it. We're fucking coyotes. We're tenacious," I said.

"I'm still amped from that set. Anybody wanna stick around and dance?" Juniper asked, shooting a glance at Rowan.

Before she'd finished the question, Otter-Pup was making eyes at a man at least twenty-years older than him, with thick arms and shitty tattoos. He wandered away from us, writhing and dancing until the man caught him around the waist and they spun off together.

"I guess Otter-Pup's down. I'll stay," Gemini said.

I loved playing music. It made my blood run hot and my body pulse. And then I crashed. Hard. I was ready to fall asleep standing up and probably would if I stuck around. "Have fun young'uns. I'm heading out. Be safe, watch out for each other, and kick that dude's ass if he tries to fuck with Otter-Pup, yeah?"

"Always, Mixi." Gemini grinned.

I gave them all quick, firm hugs and waved at Otter-Pup. He smiled and waved back. I gave the man he was dancing with a sharp glare and was happy to see his smile wilt and his aggressive, thrusting, handsy dancing tone down a touch.

On my way out, I shook hands with Lala. "Thanks."

"The Mangy Rats were amazing, as always." She smiled, but it didn't reach her eyes. There was a slump in her shoulders I hadn't seen before.

"Probably none of my business, but everything alright, Lala?"

"Fuck, but you shifters are more perceptive than my own mother."

I laughed. "Yeah well, at least the social ones are. I met a weremoose once. Girl knew right away if you were trying to fuck with her and would get pissed like no one I've ever seen. But anything else? She wouldn't spot it until and unless you screamed it in her face."

"There are were*moose*?"

I shrugged. "At least one."

"When I was a kid there were werewolves and nothing else. And not nearly as many as there are now. Mostly lived up in the mountains in tiny communities and coming in to town for supplies once in a while. Real secretive old families going back generations. Every now and again, you ran into somebody who pissed off a witch and got turned. Now there's coyotes and moose and who knows what the fuck else."

"Came a surprise to me, too." I chuckled and it came out more bitter than I intended, but if Lala noticed, she ignored it.

She lowered her voice so it was barely audible over the din of the bar. "Can I ask…?"

"How I got turned? Yeah, you can ask." I grabbed the nearest chair, swung one leg over, and sat down backwards. "Truth is, I don't know. It happened four years ago. I blacked out and woke up in a field with the Mangy Rats, who were strangers, except for Gemini, in those days. My mom always told me that the only two ways to turn into a shifter were born to it, but I wasn't, or to piss off a witch, which I definitely don't remember doing. She doesn't talk to me anymore. Real superstitious. Thinks I caught the eye of an evil witch and will bring bad luck wherever I go."

"My dad was the same way. Used to hang cats' eyes made of blown glass in every window to keep the house safe from the eyes of any passing witch. He doesn't talk to me anymore either. Found sage in my bedroom and accused me of trying to summon demons into the house."

"Yeah, I guess a witch daughter isn't much more welcome than a werecoyote if you think witchcraft is demonic. Did he make you eat raw onion on the full moon?" I asked.

"Oh god, yes. At least until I got big enough to run the fuck away. I still can't stomach onions, even cooked." She laughed and shook her head. "Things are different in the cities. Even little ones like Oak Tree Harbor, but not that different. Everybody here wants to trade with witches, but not be seen in public with us."

"Fucking city norms are the most hypocritical. But, it seems to me and my werecoyote perceptiveness that you've changed the subject. You don't have sad puppy dog eyes because people are generally disappointing. But it's okay. You don't have to tell me what's up if you don't want to, just thought you should know that I'm on to you."

She laughed dryly and sighed. "Yeah, you got me. But I'm dodging only 'cause I think you got a right to know but I don't really want to talk about it. So here it goes. Mechanical Anatomy is closing down right after the final showdown."

"What?" I shouted.

"Seems some rich shithead wants to turn it into a theater. Reported me to the city for a host of health and safety violations, most of which were true enough. I mean, there was a lot I was supposed to do before opening this place up to the public but I didn't have the money to do any of it. They're closing me down. Well, technically they *already* closed me down, but fuck 'em right? I'll keep running this thing until they drag me out."

"A theater? Like, a movie theater?" I couldn't believe it. Mechanical Anatomy was home for so many of us. We'd have to move on. No point in a punk band staying here in this backwater town if they didn't even have a venue for us to play. We'd been here six months, which was longer than I'd been anywhere since

I left home. I'd started to think Oak Tree Harbor *was* home.

"No, like a *thee-ater*. Plays, classical music, assigned seating, velvet chairs."

I looked around the bar. "No offense, Lala, but where exactly would any of that stuff fit?"

"They bought the strip mall up above, too. They're going to tear all that down. Mechanical Anatomy will be basement storage or a boiler room or something."

"That is some bullshit. I'm sorry, Lala. Anything we can do to help?"

"Not unless you can figure out who the mystery billionaire is, scare them away, and pay for a crew to come renovate this place. But hey, I had a good run here. Put on some shows folks will be talking about to their grandkids, and we're going to go out with a rad show by three of the best bands to ever play my stage. So, make sure you make it a good one."

"You know we will."

She held out her hand and I took it. She squeezed my hand tight. "It's been fun." Lala returned to the bar to mix drinks and I went out into the dark to walk home.

The night air was cool on my sweaty skin and the sky was littered with stars. Nights like this were why I liked living in smaller places instead of big cities. But, maybe it was time we headed to one of the coasts and try to catch some gigs in bigger venues. I'd done it in my teens. It was rough. I played a lot more shows, made a lot more money, but the money I made didn't go far enough save me from squatting and sleeping in my car. At least out here the weather was mild and we could set up camp outside of the city and nobody would hassle us. Besides, living in a big city now would mean budgeting for gas to get us to some woods every month for the full moon. In Oak Tree Harbor, they didn't exactly love their shifter population, but they tolerated us. Even made a few accommodations with only minimal grumbling, like keeping their pets and kids inside on the full moon just in case one of us got too close and was tempted by the animal brain crowding out the rest of our senses.

"Hey, wait up," someone said from behind me.

I turned to see R, her makeup still flawless. She wore a long black cape draped over her shoulders and fastened around her neck with a ruby studded broach in the shape of a skeletal hand. I tensed. Was she here to start trouble? Trying to scare off the competition?

I gave her a cold stare. "Hi."

She took out a pack of cigarettes and offered one to me. I shook my head. She pulled one out with her long fingers and lit it. "Y'all put on a good show tonight."

"Thanks."

"Oh come on, we're all civilized occasional canids here. That was genuine. You're good."

"You all put on a good show, too. A little glossy and melodramatic for my tastes, but still, I'm sure the goth kids were into it."

She smiled. Her perfect white teeth stood out against the darkness of her deep blue lipstick. "I'm sure they did. Just like I'm sure the punks enjoyed your set. It was hard to tell that you all are *actually* good underneath all the screaming and banging. A little histrionic for me, but hey, I do appreciate finding out there are punks out there who actually know what chords are." She gave me a wicked grin.

God, but I hated the wolves.

Her face turned serious. "I saw you talking to Lala. Did she tell you about The Mechanical Anatomy?"

I searched for some sign she was trying to fuck with me, but all I found was earnest concern. "Yeah."

"What do you think?"

"What do you mean?"

"Who do you think is behind it?" she asked.

"I don't know. I'm not sure why anyone thinks a fancy theater in Oak Tree Harbor is going to rake in the cash. The punks, metal heads, and goth kids aside, folks here are more into classic rock than art house."

"That's what I thought too. But there's signs going up in Hammond trying to sell Oak Tree Harbor as the place to move for cheap real estate. Even citing so-called urban and modern conveniences like the coming-soon Rosebud Theater."

"Meaning they're going to force everybody out, not just

Lala. It was a matter of time, I guess. It's happening all over. It's coming here sooner than I was hoping, but I figured we'd be moving on eventually."

"Who says we should just roll over and take it?" she said, her voice sharp.

"I don't know. Life, I guess. What, you think you're going to fight some big-ass corporation and the entirety of Hammond City? Most people here don't give a fuck about us or Lala or The Mechanical Anatomy. They'll be starting up tourist bureaus and hotels within a month."

"Until they get forced out, too."

"That's the way it works. The rich people scare off or force out the black folks, the trans people and the queers, the shifters, any witches who won't cater to them, and then the rest of the poors and middlings get booted to make way for condominiums. And that last group never seems to see it coming or want to listen to the rest of us when we tell them what's up."

"So, we should just roll over and take it? Aren't punks supposed to be all hardcore, never back down, switchblade in your boot, damn the man, and burn it all down?"

I bristled and pressure built in my gums as my coyote teeth threatened to burst free. I took a deep breath, then another, until the pressure disappeared. I turned to fire a retort, but R was stripping off her clothes. My face warmed. I wasn't uncomfortable with nudity—the coyotes shifted in front of each other all the time and when we were home it was a constant battle to convince Otter-Pup to ever wear clothes—but R wasn't my pack. I closed my eyes.

She laughed, a throaty, growling sound. I opened my eyes just in time to see her drop to all fours. Fur rolled out of her skin in black and silver waves, rippling down her back to her ass. She howled. The sound was answered by wolves somewhere in the distance. Her packmates? Regular wolves? She grabbed her dropped clothes between her teeth and she was off, racing through the edges of the city to the fields outside.

CHAPTER 2

"Welcome home." I sipped my coffee and watched my small campfire burn as Juniper and Rowan stumbled into camp. Rowan's black mullet was sticking out in every direction and matted with twigs and nettles; his dark brown skin was bruised with bite and suck marks.

Juniper blushed. "What are you doing up already?"

"It's one in the afternoon," I said.

"Oops. Well, I withdraw the question. Gem and Otter-Pup make it home yet?"

"Yup. Gemini went to bed and Otter-Pup is gardening."

"Doesn't that kid sleep?" Rowan asked.

I laughed. "You know Otter-Pup's got two settings: sleep for twenty-hours or sleep for two. There's bagels on the counter, bacon in the pan, and fresh coffee in a pot on the fire."

"You are a god, Mixi." Juniper grabbed a plate and shoveled food onto it.

Gemini's sleeping bag squirmed like a caterpillar until their head popped out. "I think I smell coffee."

"Your nose is correct. Could you grab Otter-Pup from the garden? Something I need to talk to y'all about," I said.

They yawned and stretched, then nodded and shuffled off to Otter-Pup's pride and joy. A plot of land the size of a school gym with bright green vegetables sprouting from the rich, dark soil.

Otter-Pup and Gemini returned to the campsite. Otter-Pup's skin was flushed and slicked with sweat. Despite all of our late night, we beamed with energy and good spirits. "What's the news?"

"Grab food and coffee first, if you want it," I said.

Otter-Pup wandered over to the long, wooden, graffiti covered table that I'd scavenged for us last year. And by scavenged, I do mean that I drove by a licensed government run campground and threw it in the back of my truck during the winter while no one was around. It served as our countertop. Otter-Pup grabbed a bagel and smeared it with peanut butter, while Gemini grabbed the pot of coffee that was being kept warm over the fire.

When everyone was seated and eating, I told them what Lala had said.

"That's bullshit," Gemini said, "They can't take The Mechanical Anatomy away. This place will die, just some hollow shell filled with dad rock and tourists."

"That's the idea, I think. Dad rock and tourists bring in the money but broke ass crust punks just bring in more broke ass crust punks," Juniper said.

"Yeah, but we make this place cool. It's why any of them want to come here in the first place," Gemini said.

I held up my hands. "We're not here to argue the ills of capitalism, I think we're all on the same page there. But what are we going to do?" I'd spent all night thinking about R and her challenge. *Aren't punks supposed to be fighters?* But what was there to fight? A handful of us couldn't stop the march of hotels, spas, and shopping malls any more than we could stop the coming of a storm.

"I guess we could head for Atalburg. An old bandmate moved there, says she's doing alright. Or we could head for one of the big cities," Rowan said.

"And what? Run through the streets every full moon? Unless you're rich, shifters get forced out of the big cities. I guess Atalburg might work. They've got a decent music scene at least," Gemini said.

"Or we could stay here," I said.

Otter-Pup looked up from his bagel, his big eyes round and hopeful. I took a deep breath. That look of his was the worst. I was his pack leader and his band leader and I knew he trusted me to figure this out for all of them.

Gemini chewed their lower lip. "We could let them have The Mechanical Anatomy and start a new bar. Or, convince Lala to do it, running a bar seems like more work than I'm up for. Hell, it's music. If we can run an extension cord far enough, we could play out here if we have to."

I nodded, relieved they'd taken a little bit of the burden off me. "That's a good point. The Mechanical Anatomy doesn't own the music scene in Oak Tree Harbor, no matter how much we all love Lala. And maybe with enough support, she could reopen somewhere else. We could also try and find out who it is that bought it."

Juniper raised a perfectly sculpted eyebrow. "And do what? Convince them to change their minds?" Her teeth slid down from her gums and she snapped at the air.

"I'm not ruling that out and I like the enthusiasm. But let's start with something less messy. Like research. We don't know who it is that bought it. Probably some boring real estate developer or bank. But we don't know that for sure. Besides, boring business people probably have the creepiest skeletons in their closets, right? If we figure it out, that could give us some ideas about what to do about it," I said.

Gemini's face split into a grin. "I guess that's my job."

"Hell yeah, get to it, you mangy coyote." Juniper winked at them and they blushed.

Seeing the look on Gemini's face I realized I had been wrong. They hadn't been Juniper and Rowan's unwitting third wheel last night. They had been their very aware third wheel because they were afraid of Juniper's intensifying relationship with Rowan. How had I missed that? I'd have to talk to Gemini later about it. If Otter-Pup didn't beat me to it.

"Thanks, Gemini. Let me know what you find out. But, it'll probably have to wait until after the full-moon. We'll all be occupied tonight and you don't focus any better than I do during the day leading up to it," I said.

They nodded. "Seriously. If I didn't have my pride I'd spend all day eating bacon and maybe scrounging through the garbage can to eat trash. But I'll see if I can't figure out anything today so we can go bash skulls or growl menacingly or send threatening letters from fake lawyers as soon as we can."

The sun drooped as Gemini typed and cursed at their computer. I, and the others, dozed, letting the sun warm us right down to our bones.

"I think I have something," they said.

I opened my eyes. My eyesight was now sharp and crisp, but drained of color. Thrilling smells wafted from everything around me. Rich fat on the bacon, warm, musky sweat on my pack mates, even the sweet rot of asparagus stalks and orange peels in the garbage. Night was drawing closer and I was starting to shift whether I wanted to or not. Soon we'd all be furry.

"What did you find?" Even my voice was changing. Higher and barking.

"The company that bought The Mechanical Anatomy doesn't exist as far as I can tell. There's a sale registered with the city, but the named buyer doesn't have a web page and isn't listed by any licensing agency or business bureau I can find. But I did a lot of digging around, utilizing my towering intelligence, and many fancy tricks that I assure you were very impressive even if you would understand them. I found an address finally. It's a local place, but I haven't heard of the street. Mortar Way. Any of you know it?"

We all shook our heads.

"That's it. That's all I can find. I guess whoever bought it doesn't want to be found, which is interesting. But they had to put down an address or the city wouldn't recognize the sale," Gemini said.

"Good work. We'll check it out. Tomorrow, if we're up to it," I said.

They glanced up at the sky and smiled, their face elongated into a muzzle and their eyes reflected the light from the dying campfire. "Time to run," they said.

I felt it too. My skin was too tight, too slow, too naked. Fur rippled across my arms and my back ached to bend and fold to all fours. Around me, the others were shifting. Gregarious yips and barks filled the air and my brain cleared. My thoughts went simple and clever. Uncomplicated by the bullshit of human life.

I barked and took off running, my pack racing at my heels, into the long grass that told me stories in smells. A rabbit had hopped through here, eating clover. A mole snuffled just beneath the earth and pulled grubs from the soil. Birds flitted and pecked at the thistle seeds and each other. And somewhere, not too far, were wolves.

My muscles tensed. Wolves were a dangerous opportunity. They killed us, and not just for food. Sometimes they left us lying dead for no other reason than not wanting to share food. But they also killed *other* things and left tantalizing remains behind. We'd stay far from the wolves for now, but we'd be back to follow their scent and learn if they'd had any luck with the hunt.

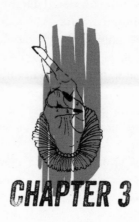

CHAPTER 3

I woke up naked in a field, my belly full, and blood smeared and caked across my face. I groaned and rolled over onto my side to hide from the glaring sun. My mouth was parched and tasted like meat and old garbage.

The day after a full moon shift felt like the worst hangover I'd ever had. Like I'd gotten drunk on sugary cocktails chased with tequila shots. I sat up and groaned as my head throbbed like a pissed off little demon was inside my skull, jabbing my brain with his pitchfork every time I moved.

Gemini's arm stuck out of a bush nearby. They grimaced and swatted a spider off their face, rolling out into the sun. I found Juniper and Rowan still asleep, curled up together like pups. In the inhibition of a total shift, they lost the control to hide their new relationship. Where was Otter-Pup?

I sat up, ignoring the waves of pain and nausea. My heart beat faster until I saw him, curled up in a ball against my back. If he'd been any closer, he'd have been sleeping on top of me.

His eyes fluttered and he yawned. Then he winced. "Ow, my poor head."

Gemini gave a weak laugh. "If someone wants to just knock me unconscious until tomorrow, I won't protest."

I climbed to my feet. "Come on, everybody. We can't stay

26

here. Folks here might be cool enough to give us the full moon to do our thing, but not if one of their poor, delicate children stumbled over us naked and bloody in a field at noon. We don't need another situation like what happened in Felton."

"Fucking prudes," Gemini grumbled, but they did what I said.

We stumbled back to our campsite, every one of us an exhausted, aching, mess. I grabbed a water bottle and chugged it down, feeling moderately more functional, and then slipped on a long t-shirt and a pair of shorts before dropping into a heap next to the cold fire pit. The others wandered to their respective tents in search of clothes, water, and peaceful darkness. My stomach was full to bursting, and yet I wanted food that wasn't scavenged raw meat or stolen garbage. I didn't even like to contemplate what I ate when I went full coyote. I knew the type of shit we ate.

I could fit some coffee in my stomach at least. God, coffee sounded like heaven right now. But that would involve starting the fire. And enough focus to make sure it didn't burn or boil over. That sounded way too hard.

I dozed off, the warmth of the sun soothing muscles that ached from shifting and running all night.

When I opened my eyes again, I felt better. Not great. But as good as I was going to feel until I put some coffee, bread, and vegetables in my stomach. I got the fire going again. I plucked tomatoes from Otter-Pup's garden and dug through the box of food pantry finds we'd collected. I chopped up onions and squash, drizzling them in oil and sprinkling them with salt and pepper, then combined them with the asparagus in a square of tin foil. I placed the foil-wrapped vegetables in the homemade steel basket that hung over the fire to cook. I filled the pot with water and placed it over the fire as well.

Once the water was boiling, I poured it slowly over a coffee filter fixed to a tall, narrow jar with a rubber band. I took off the filter and set the grounds aside to dry. We were running low and would probably have to reuse some grounds before we managed to snag some more coffee. Then I took the vegetables off the fire and divided them into four equal piles.

"There's food and coffee if anyone's awake," I said loud enough to be heard inside all the tents, but hopefully not so loud as to wake up anyone lucky enough to still be in a sound sleep.

Juniper's tent flap opened and she and Rowan climbed out, not pretending anymore. That was probably for the best. As Gemini came out of their own tent and glanced at them, their face wilted with hurt and sadness. I should still talk to them about it. Love could be a real minefield.

Otter-Pup climbed out of his tent, his eyes clear, and his hair somehow looking good. I hadn't been a werecoyote at eighteen, but I did remember how much faster I bounced back from late nights, liquor, and drugs at that age. It was probably the same. I'd resent him for it if he weren't such a sweet, thoughtful, elfin little weirdo.

They dropped together on the soft grass and I handed everyone a plate of vegetables and a cup of coffee. We passed around a loaf of stale bread and everyone tore off a chunk, eating in silence while the caffeine and vitamins did their work.

When everyone had finished and was sipping their coffee with half-closed eyes and blissful faces, I cleared my throat. All eyes turned to me.

"What we were talking about yesterday…"

For a moment I was met with blank stares, the overwhelming haze of a full moon driving out other memories. Then I saw it click.

"Shit, right. The Mechanical Anatomy and the mystery buyer," Rowan said.

"Do you all feel up to going on an adventure to check out that address Gemini found?" I asked.

Gemini and Juniper groaned.

"Come on. It's for Lala and The Mechanical Anatomy and freedom and love and found family and punk and art and whatever," Otter-Pup said.

Rowan laughed. "Well said."

"I'm going. I'd like at least one of you to come with me in case there's trouble or I need a look-out. But, it's probably not going to take five of us, so if anybody wants to stay here, that's fine," I said.

"Fuck no. We're all going. If we save The Mechanical Anatomy and Lala and the music scene in this weird little city, I want credit," Otter-Pup said.

Gemini chuckled. "Yeah. Same. I'm coming."

Juniper tilted back her coffee cup. "I'm coming, too."

Rowan nodded.

"Alright, well, secure your stuff and let's go," I said.

CHAPTER 4

The house on Mortar Way was a sight. Steel mesh fencing surrounded it, with holes too small to get a foothold, and the top was ringed with wicked looking barbed wire. The walls of the house were painted with huge, disembodied chicken legs. A rusting rooster weathervane squeaked as it swung gently in the wind and the distinctive odor of chicken shit, hay, and dusty feathers hung heavy in the air. A flock of chickens surrounded the house; pecking, clucking, and chasing one another.

"Holy fuck. *This* is who bought The Mechanical Anatomy? How does someone who lives in a scary nest of chicken hoarding afford to do something like that?" Gemini asked.

"We don't know for sure. The address might be a fake," I said.

"If so, they went through a lot of trouble to hide a fake address," Gemini said.

"We won't know for sure until we figure out a way inside," Otter-Pup said.

A low, throaty woman's voice came from behind me. "Took y'all long enough."

I turned to see R, dressed in casual goth with tight black jeans tucked into combat boots bearing steel bats on the sides. Two wolves flanked her: the guitar player, a tall, lithe black woman named Bee who was still dressed in black leather and had purple woven into her long locs, and the electric violinist, Ebo, a genderqueer with brown skin and a thick black beard threaded with blood red beads.

"I see the wolves came dressed practically as always," I said.

R smiled, her purple lipstick perfect and dabbed with a touch of glitter. "As did the coyotes. Ten pounds of hairspray and zero pounds of tools." She held up a tool box in one hand and wire cutters in the other.

I glared at her and she smiled wider, deepening the dimples left behind by the cheek piercings she wasn't currently wearing.

"Were you expecting us?" Otter-Pup asked.

"I asked your pack leader to consider not tucking tail and running away. I'm glad Mixi decided to stand up after all," R said.

Rowan stepped forward but I put my arm in front of him.

"We have the same goal here. How about we get on with this bit of breaking and entering before someone gets suspicious?" I said.

R bowed her head slightly. "Perhaps you and your pack should stay outside and keep watch. I don't think we need eleven people for this."

"Not a chance. Your pack can wait outside," I said.

Three other wolves joined the group. Maezi, the drummer, a woman so pale I could see the blue of her veins through her skin. KC, the keyboard player, a heavily tattooed man with long black hair and olive skin. And Cole, their bassist, with natural red hair so bright it made Juniper's look pale, and a crystal dermal piercing under their right eye like a teardrop.

Otter-Pup wiggled his fingers at KC who bit his lip, blushed, and looked away.

I forced down an amused chuckle. Otter-Pup mentioned they had a fling. Any of the other coyotes and I might be concerned about split loyalties or opening us up to sabotage right before the Battle of the Bands showdown. But Otter-Pup was so kind-hearted, mischievous, and charming that he could half-murder me in my sleep and I'd probably not only forgive him, but assume he had a good reason to do it.

Bee cleared her throat. "With respect, R, we really do need to hurry it up. How about two wolves and two coyotes go inside?

The rest of us will spread out and keep watch."

R turned and nodded to her. "Always the diplomat, Bee. And of course, you're right. Maezi and I will go. What about your people, Mixi?"

I looked at the coyotes. We all seemed so small standing next to the wolves. "I'll go. Gemini, you found the place, you get first dibs on coming or staying."

"Shit, of course I'll go. There might be a fight to be had." They grinned.

"Alright. You have the tools, lead the way." I waved to R.

She leaned down and snipped wires until she'd made a hole big enough for her and Maezi to fit through, which meant it was more than big enough for me and Gemini. R wiggled through, her round butt pressing against her tight pants. Otter-Pup winked at me as my face warmed. He sidled up to KC who looked happy to have him there. I rolled my eyes and followed R and Maezi. Gemini slipped through behind me.

"We'll go around back. You two go to the front. Cole and KC already rang the bell to see if anyone was home, but they might have just been ignoring us. If someone is there, pretend to be selling candy bars for your school band trip or something and then yell," R said.

"School band trip? You are the most annoying person I have ever met. And I once played a show at a frat house after they booked my band by accident thinking we were strippers," I said.

R covered her mouth to catch a laugh. "Oh my god. Can we get drinks together sometime? Because I definitely want to hear that story."

Her smile was genuine and I found my heart racing. Fuck. I was not going to develop a crush on a werewolf. "Um—uh yeah."

We split up. Gemini and I skulked to the front door. I snorted. Even the door knocker was a brass chicken. Who were these people, Old MacDonald? I knocked. No one came to the door. I knocked again. It was still silent.

Gemini peered through the window and turned to me, shaking their head. Their ears elongated and turned furry and pointy. They pressed the shifted ear against the window and gestured at me to knock again. I pounded as hard as I could and they winced. After a long minute they stood up straight.

"There's nobody in there. Unless they sleep like the dead," they said.

"Alright, well let's find a way inside and hope this place doesn't belong to Dracula." I stepped aside and let Gemini do their thing. The door looked flimsy, so I could probably bust in with an old credit card, but Gemini was the expert at getting into anything people didn't want them inside. Houses, computer files, grocery stores after-hours, and on one notable occasion, the low-security jail and drunk tank in Felton.

Something stabbed my calf just above the edge of my boot. I shouted and looked down.A chicken stood at my feet. It bobbed its head forward, again stabbing me in the shin with its beak. I kicked at it, careful not to actually hurt it, just enough to push it away. It stood bobbing its head and studying me. I reached down and touched my calf. My fingers came away red.

"Fuck, that chicken just bit me," I said.

Gemini continued working on the door. "Chickens don't bite, Mixi."

"Fine. It pecked me hard enough to draw blood."

"Hold on. I'm almost in," they said, their voice distant and distracted.

I turned back to eye the chicken. It hopped up the steps. I tried to nudge it back and it darted forward with its beak, pecking my leg again. It bobbed to the left and then darted to the right to peck viciously at my right shin. The goddamn chicken was feinting and using strategy against me.

I would not be outsmarted by something with a brain the size of a lentil. I retreated towards the house until my back was against the wall. I crouched low and shifted enough of my body that I would smell strongly of coyote. Patchy fur sprouted from my arms and my teeth slid out of the gums. The bird didn't seem to care. It trotted up and started pecking at me again.

I jumped out of the way, moving closer to Gemini. It paused a moment, tilting its head side to side, watching me.

I swear to God, its eyes glowed pale green.

The chicken spread its wings and hopped towards me, its

chubby body bouncing in what should be an adorable way across the porch. As if it had signaled the others, a wave of clucking and fluttering filled the air as the rest of the flock mobbed me. Wings beat against my legs and a bird threw its body against the back of my knees, knocking me flat on my ass. Sensing weakness, they swarmed over me. Taloned feet and feathers beat at my face until I couldn't see a thing. I waved my arms to drive them away but their beaks ripped through the skin. Trapped beneath the cloud of enraged poultry, I curled into a ball and wrapped my arms over my head as their sharp beaks tore at my clothes and skin.

Behind me, over the din of wings and clucking, Gemini yelled. I pulled myself up on all fours, but I couldn't see through the pissed off chickens. I took a deep breath and crawled through the sea of feathers until I could pull myself to my feet. They pecked and shoved against my legs and knees, but I was ready for those tricky bastards this time. I walked backwards, towards the sound of Gemini's voice, kicking at the birds until I fell through the open door. They slammed it shut behind me.

One bird managed to come through with me. The same green-eyed demon creature that attacked me first.

"I'm going to turn that goddamn bird into a chicken nugget," I shouted.

Gemini held up their hand and grabbed a heavy wool blanket off the threadbare couch, covered in yet another chicken pattern. They tossed it over the bird and scooped it up. I looked around for some place to put it. The living room was small and comfortable. Normal in an "obsessed with chickens" sort of way, with no obvious spots to stash a furious, cursed chicken. A narrow hallway lined with three doors ran behind us. I pointed.

They nodded, opened the first door, and tossed the squawking bundle inside. They slammed the door shut just as the bird threw its body against it in a dull, feathery whump.

"Wow. I figured coyotes could at least handle not having their asses kicked by a few chickens," R said.

R leaned against the wall on the other side of the living room. Behind her was a large cupboard and a dining table. I caught a glimpse of myself in the mirror hanging from the cupboard door. Streaks of blood ran down my face, hair stuck in every direction—and not in an intentional way—and feathers and chicken shit gunked everywhere.

"For your information, apart from the full moon and the day leading up to it, I'm a vegetarian. I won't kill a chicken no matter how much of an asshole it is," I said.

"So, you're telling me that your threat to turn that one into a chicken nugget was completely empty? No wonder it didn't back off," she said.

It took me a moment to realize she was joking. I wasn't in the mood. I had just been mobbed by the most pissed-off, freaky-smart chickens in the world. So, I ignored it. "Did you find anything yet?"

R wiggled her finger, beckoning us to follow her into the kitchen. The air was heavy with rich spices, burnt sage, and coppery blood. Bottles and dusty, leather bound books lined the shelves. None of the books had titles on the spines. I picked one up and flipped through the pages, enjoying the musty smell of old book. All handwritten. But it wasn't a journal. It looked more like a cookbook. I groaned. "A witch."

"Witches. From the handwriting, the four cauldrons on the counter, and different style amulets hanging on the walls, I'd guess that there's more than one living here and doing spell work," R said.

"Well, check you out, Detective Wolf," I said.

She gave me a crooked half smile. "I was really into witchcraft before the werewolf thing. Didn't have much natural aptitude, but I know damn near everything about potions and spells you could learn without having an actual witch apprentice you." She picked up a bottle and sniffed it. She wrinkled her nose and put it down. "Blood mixed with sulfur, that's some dark shit."

"I figured all goths had a witch phase," I said.

"What, you didn't? Come on, Mixi, what's more punk DIY than witchcraft?" she said.

I laughed. "Yeah, okay. I had a witchcraft phase, too. I was never good at sitting still long enough to learn much more than how to make stink bombs to throw in the middle school gymnasium, though."

Gemini cleared their throat. "So, what does a coven want with The Mechanical Anatomy?"

R coughed, caught bantering, and her cheeks reddened. "I'm not sure. Maybe it's just coincidence that they're witches and they just happen to also dabble in real estate. I mean, cursing your enemies and blessing yourself with good fortune is helpful in a lot of lines of work."

I raised an eyebrow. "Sure. But combined with magic that is, as you said, dark shit, that seems unlikely."

"Let's keep looking, maybe we'll find something to explain what this all about," Gemini said.

We fanned out. R dug through the cabinets, Maezi explored the living room, and Gemini and I went down the hall to check out the other rooms. The chicken clucked and pecked at the door Gemini had locked it behind.

"Let's just call that room a dead end. It was a bathroom, probably nothing too incriminating in there, right?" Gemini said.

"Agreed. I don't really want to wrestle a demonic chicken, or a witch's familiar, or whatever that bird is."

I opened the door at the farthest end of the hall and looked inside. It was dark inside. I reached for the light switch, but found only smooth empty wall. I shifted my eyes so I could see in the dim light. Heavy, black blankets blocked the windows and an unmade bed sat in the middle of the room.

"Everything okay?" I called down the hall to Gemini.

They peeked their head out. "Yup, you?"

I nodded and proceeded inside the room. It smelled strange. Musky like animals in a barn or a zoo, and sickly sweet like fruit left to rot on the ground of an orchard. I opened the drawer of the nightstand and found more books. I flipped through them and stopped when one caught my eye: *Vitoriol's Guide to Ritual Animal Magic*. I opened it and skimmed the pages. Inside the cover, someone had written: *For Jeza*.

The book wasn't a catalogue of spells, more like a witch's theoretical memoir. The first chapter discussed the process and ethics of turning an animal into a familiar. As far as my understanding went, that was difficult, but typical enough as far as advanced witchcraft. But familiars carried messages, added their power to spell work, or allowed the witch to see through its eyes. They didn't attack people like rabid guard dogs or have glowing eyes.

The next chapter was more promising. It discussed various methods of controlling animals. First, through the reanimation of corpses. According to the author, that was difficult magic to control for more than a few hours, often leaving behind a vengeful ghost with a vendetta against the witch who'd raised it, as soon as its body rotted too much and could no longer retain the animal's spirit.

I skipped ahead. The next chapter described Vitoriol's experiments taking an animal's will and replacing it with his own, effectively making the creature an extension of himself, without needing a corpse to reanimate. He described performing the magic on a pet cat. The cat had taken to wandering out of his yard until he performed the spell to replace the cat's will with his own. Afterwards, the cat became a sentinel of his house. Never leaving, providing warning of approaching strangers, and attacking only those animals and insects that were in the house, leaving birds and squirrels outside alone.

Well, that was creepy as all hell. Poor cat.

He didn't write out each step of the ritual. Which was probably for the best. I didn't really want all the details in my head. There were magic words that had to be performed in exactly the right way. It required bloodletting to bind the witch and the creature. Because of course. It wasn't dark magic if it wasn't disgusting.

Someone had scrawled notes into the margins next to this section:

Tell me the steps, you coward.

Vitoriol was a musician. Words + tone + rhythm = music.

Binding magic as described on p 211 of Marisol's Diary is an image drawn in blood.

Experiment worked. Replaced will of squirrel. Effective. Drowned itself on command.

Could it work on more than one animal if the witch were in harmony with multiple animals? Confirmed. Chickens. One becomes the vessel of the witch's will and others like living zombies that respond to its call. Good enough.

Shifters?????

Turned enough for final test. Hope this fucking works.

I stared at the pages trying to make sense of the notes. I had an idea and if I was right, we were all fucked. I ripped the pages out of the book and ran out of the room.

Gemini stepped out of the room they'd searched, their face pale and eyes wide.

"Are you okay?"

"Yeah. There's just four dead chickens in there. It–" They shuddered. "It looks like one was killed by a person and the other three killed each other."

"There is some evil shit happening in here. Come on, we need to grab R and Maezi and get out of here." I wrapped my arm around their shoulders and gave them a quick hug. The feel of a pack member calmed my nerves.

As I stepped into the kitchen, R grabbed my arm. "KC just texted. A car is coming up the road, it might be them, we have to go."

We ran out the front door and R closed it behind us. I shimmied under the fence, followed by Gemini, then Maezi, and R.

R stopped and jerked. "Shit, I'm stuck."

I knelt beside her and untangled a bit of metal from her shirt. The skin underneath was bleeding, but not badly. She wriggled the rest of the way out.

"Wait, hand me the wire cutters," I said.

Cole looked puzzled, but did what I said without argument. I trimmed off the bit of fence that had caught R's clothes, bits of blood dotting the sharp tip and handed it to her. "Don't want to leave blood at a witch's house."

R smiled. "Good thinking."

"Now let's get out of here," Otter-Pup said.

R held up her hand. "I think we need to keep watch on this place. Mixi?"

"I agree. I don't have time to tell you all what I found just yet, but we should keep an eye on what's going on here," I said.

R nodded. "Mixi and I will stay and keep watch. We'll fill each other in, then I'll fill the wolves in."

"And I'll fill in the rest of you. Is that alright?"

Gemini, Otter-Pup, Rowan, and Juniper all nodded.

"Good, go on back to camp and get some sleep. Rowan, do you mind taking a watch tomorrow? Meet us here and I'll explain everything to you first."

"Of course, Mixi."

"Same thing to you, KC."

KC nodded and the two packs left us alone.

R pointed out a thick limbed oak tree. "You up for a little climb, coyote?"

I studied the tree she pointed to. If we could get up to the fourth branch, we'd have a good view of the house while still being hidden by branches. As a bonus, another smaller, gnarled branch hung close enough to act as a back rest. My ass would be sore, but it was doable. The trouble would be getting a hold of that first branch to climb.

"Not a problem." I strode to the tree, trying to look more confident than I was. I really wasn't looking to embarrass myself in front of R. I reached up, my fingertips grazed the branch.

R cleared her throat and started to say something. When I looked at her, she held up her hands and shook her head. "You got this."

I jumped and caught the branch. It was thick and my hands didn't wrap around it. I tried to pull myself up. I was tough and scrappy, but not given to doing pullups in my spare time. My hands slipped off the branch and I fell back to the ground. At least I kept my feet. My dignity was dented but at least fifty percent intact.

"Do you need some help?" she asked.

I glared at the traitorous branch.

"I don't think it's going to come down any lower just because you're pissed at it," R said.

There was nothing else for me to do. "Fine. I'll take a boost."

She smiled and I was grateful to her for not giving me more shit. I'm wasn't sure I'd have been as gracious if our positions were reversed. She came up behind me and put her hands on either side of my waist. She smelled like sweat and campfire smoke and her body was soft and warm against my back. I swallowed a knot in my throat. Nope. I was not going to develop a crush on a werewolf. That was *not* happening. Otter-Pup could flirt and fuck with whomever he liked. He was a sweet, soft-hearted, horny as hell, cinnamon roll of a person. I was the pack leader. It was different.

"Alright, jump on three. One. Two. Three."

As I jumped, R's strong hands lifted me high enough to grip the branch and use the stronger muscles of my shoulders and back to pull myself the rest of the way up. The other branches were closer together and I made my way to the branch that looked out over the witch's house. R followed with irritating ease and grace and sat beside me. I became acutely aware of her skin as she settled in, our arms and thighs pressed against one another.

"Must have been a false alarm. If they were driving up the street, they'd have been here by now," I said.

"Must have been. So, what was it you found?" she asked.

For a second I forgot what she was talking about. Then I remembered and pulled the torn, now wrinkled, pages from my pocket and handed them to her.

She unfolded them and read in silence. Her lips tightened and her jaw clenched.

"What do you think?" I knew what I thought was going on, but I wanted confirmation that I wasn't being overly imaginative.

"The spell to control animals involves music and one of them 'turned enough' for a final test of this spell. They're talking about shifters. First they turn people into shifters and then with this spell they can control us. At least, in our animal forms. Hopefully not in our human forms. But then, maybe they could force us into our animal forms. Huh. Well, none of those possibilities are good ones."

I nodded, relieved that she'd read the same thing I did, and terrified by its implications. "They're going to try and turn us into mindless things like those chickens so they can make us do whatever they want. But what does that have to do with buying The Mechanical Anatomy?"

"They bought it to turn it into a big theater. If this final test works, or has already worked, they want a bigger audience."

"It's someone who has played at The Mechanical Anatomy, then." I thought about it. "But wait, that doesn't make sense, my entire pack turned into werecoyotes in Felton, not in Oak Tree Harbor."

"Yeah. Three of us were turned after a show in Hammond. The others were turned in different cities and at different times."

"Someone in the scene then. Do you know any musicians named Jeza? Or can you think of anybody you've seen before coming to Oak Tree Harbor?"

"You mean, besides you?"

I tilted my head to the side. "What?"

She laughed. "You know you cock your head to the side just like a confused puppy? It's adorable. Yeah, I saw you play in Felton four years ago. Your new band is a hell of a lot better, by the way. But after they ran you out of town, we hightailed it fast before someone could spot us too."

"I had no idea you were part of that scene."

"Makes sense. I collected my pack over the last few years and my band in those days was also not nearly as good as Dead and Disorderly. We got a lot of beer bottles thrown at us. No reason we'd have stood out." Her voice had a tinge of something, embarrassment maybe.

I cleared my throat awkwardly. "Well that's one hell of a coincidence. I promise, I'm not a witch and neither is any of my pack. Gemini could make you think they were with their computer and lock picking skills, but they came by those the old fashioned, dishonest way."

She laughed and the uncomfortable moment was gone. "Bee does some healing magic, but apart from the wolf moon, uh sorry, is that like, species-ist? Apart from the full moon, she's a vegan and mind-fucking chickens would probably leave her in tears. I make her watch nature documentaries monthly to remind her that when she's a wolf, eating deer or whatever is a natural apex predator thing. You two might get along."

I thought back on the nights I'd played at The Mechanical Anatomy. "Baba Yaga and Tricky Bitches seemed kind of familiar. I don't remember ever seeing them play before and I got a witch vibe from them for sure."

R frowned. "You know I had the same feeling. A weird déjà vu. For the life of me, I couldn't place where and why I knew them."

CHAPTER 5

After about an hour, a group of four people walked up the road. I leaned forward and shifted my eyes to get a better view. One flipped a switch. The gate swung open and they walked up the sidewalk to the house. The chickens parted and appeared to bow. Which was weird as shit. My calf throbbed where they'd pecked me as if echoing my irritation at the suddenly respectful, creepy chickens.

All four appeared to be in their thirties or early forties. They dressed in nondescript clothes: jeans, sweatshirts, and baggy sweaters. One had hair pulled back in a ponytail, another wore a beanie, and the last two had short, masculine style haircuts. Nothing about them was familiar except that they looked like anyone you might pass in the aisle at the grocery store.

I leaned back, disappointed. "I don't know any of them, do you?"

R squinted and shook her head. "I don't. Well, so much for our theory. I was getting excited about it, too."

"Same. I guess we'll have to keep this stakeout going." I leaned back against the tree branch behind us, settling in for what looked like it was going to be a long night.

R reached into her back pocket and pulled out a silver flask with a vampire bat etched into the front. She opened it, took a sip, and passed it to me. Never one to turn down free booze, I took it. Cheap bourbon burned and warmed in a pleasant splash down my throat.

"So, how'd you gather your pack?" R asked.

"Gemini and I were staying in Felton for a bit. One night we saw a show at the Pine Box, I'm guessing you know it."

R nodded.

"I don't really know what happened. Lots of bands played that night but I hardly remember any of them. Like I dreamed the whole thing. I woke up naked in a field, covered in blood and surrounded by Gemini and three complete strangers all in the same condition as me. There was a lot of panic. I thought Gemini was going to beat the shit out of Rowan, thinking he had something to do with it. But I got everybody calmed down and we figured out that the same thing happened to all of us. Didn't know we were werecoyotes yet."

"Those first shifts are like that. None of us remembered anything that happened either. Like getting black out drunk in the worst way."

"It wasn't until after we got chased out of Felton that we figured out what was happening and managed to get control of ourselves. Luckily nobody got hurt in the meantime. Us or any norms."

"Same thing happened to us, more or less. I picked up KC, Cole, and Maezi in different cities. But Bee and Ebo got turned at the same time I did. They were in a band together. We were all at a show in Hammond, which is where I'm from. We woke up together, naked and bloody in a goddamn zoo."

"Holy shit, a *zoo*?"

She laughed softly. "Yup. I think they called the particular exhibit we were in the 'Blue Lagoon.' We all got chased out of town for being devil worshippers. The popular theory in town was we got high on drugs and satanic music, lost our minds, and started cutting up zoo animals. Bee was an absolute disaster thinking she killed a bunch of flamingos. Though, I'm not sure if she felt more guilty that she went into a zoo for any other reason than animal liberation."

I grinned. "You're right. I think I might like Bee."

"I don't regret any of it. I mean, I got a lot of rage at this being something that was done to us without our consent. And if I could do it again, I'd leave the zoo animals out of it. But, I like being a werewolf. I have family now in a way I never did before."

"I know what you mean. I wouldn't trade Otter-Pup, Juniper, and Rowan for anything. Even Gemini is more my family now. I knew them before but we were just friends. Now they're my sibling."

"You're a good pack leader, Mixi. Different than me. More democratic, but still very protective of them. I like that about you. I'm not so good at letting other people take the reins. Before this, I was a bouncer. I'm used to just telling people what to do and either they do it or I get to throw them out."

I turned and studied her. "A bouncer?"

"What, you don't think I'm scary enough?" She flexed an impressively muscular arm and bared her teeth at me.

I feigned terror until we both lost it and started laughing. I covered my mouth. "Shit. We are the absolute worst at stakeouts."

She passed me her flask again and I let the bourbon warm my belly. We sat in silence. A warm breeze tossed strands of her hair against my cheek, but I didn't complain. If I was being honest, I didn't want her to feel like she had to move away from me. The witches stayed in the house. There was no shouting and no one called the police, though they must know given their guard chicken was locked in the bathroom, that someone had been inside.

Next to me, R dozed. Her head dropped against my shoulder. Afraid she'd fall from the tree if she got too relaxed, I put an arm around her shoulders to keep her steady. My heart raced and my palms sweat like a teenager. After a few minutes, I realized she was awake again. Her breathing no longer languid and sleepy, she burrowed closer into my side. I stopped breathing entirely for at least a minute.

"Mixi?" she said.

I coughed. "Yes?"

"Can I kiss you?"

My chest tightened and my heart raced. "Yes." My voice came

out hoarse and choked.

She sat up so that we were face to face. I was struck by how beautiful her eyes were. Soft, warm, like rich dark brown velvet. She put one hand on the back of my neck and pulled me in. Our lips met and hers were soft and tasted a little like coconut. The kiss deepened and I drew her lower lip into my mouth, sucking it gently and releasing it. Her hand curled and tightened her grip on my short hair. I traced my hands down her back, stopping at the bare skin of her lower back. I wanted to dive in, hold her tight to me, and never let go. But we parted. Her beautiful eyes glimmering and hungry.

Fuck. I definitely had a crush on a werewolf.

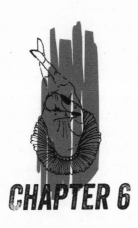

CHAPTER 6

Rand I didn't see a damn thing happening in the witches' house. If they were up to something, they were being very quiet and not doing it anywhere near any of the open windows. We spent more time than we should have making out, but only for one-minute intervals, then we went back to our stakeout, so I was pretty sure nothing real big happened. KC and Rowan arrived only five minutes apart. When we climbed down from the tree, I only protested a little when R held out her hand to help me down from the last branch.

Together we explained what we'd found and what we suspected. KC's eyes widened as we explained and Rowan stood in stony faced, angry silence.

"That's fucked up," he said when I finished talking. Of my pack, Rowan was the least at peace with what we were, so his anger was expected and probably something I'd have to prod him to talk about later.

"You two keep watch for the next few hours and we'll send someone to relieve you. Did you bring food?" I asked.

They both nodded.

"And your phones? If you see something, call us both," R said.

"Got it." KC gave Rowan a skeptical look and then forced a smile.

"Be nice," I warned Rowan.

He held up his hands and smiled. "I'm always nice."

I shot him one last warning glance and turned to leave. It was true that he was usually a calm, kind-hearted person. But, when Rowan felt like he or someone he cared about had been, or was about to be hurt, he was not the calmest. Part of the reason we were run out of Felton was our lack of control when we shifted, but it was also because, imbued with his new strength, Rowan broke his sister's abusive boyfriend's jaw. A move I normally would have applauded him for, but he did it with his entire face shifted into a coyote and in the middle of a busy shopping mall. I'd left that part out when I told the story to R. I was beginning to like her. Okay I was in deep, wild, heart soaring lust with R. But if she didn't already know that part, she didn't need to be that deep in my pack's business.

We were quiet as we walked back into town. In the warm light of day, I didn't know what to say to her that wouldn't sound ridiculous. My tongue was clumsy and weighted down and every time I tried to break the silence I tripped over my words and said something inane like, "Wow, it's sunny today."

As we reached the edge of the city, R cleared her throat. "So, Mixi, I suppose we should talk about last night."

My heart hammered in my ears. Oh god, here it was, a feelings conversation. I could talk and listen to the deepest, most intense feelings with my pack, but when faced with a simple conversation with a woman I'd made out with and my entire brain ceased functioning.

"What's there to talk about?" I blurted.

R flinched. "You know, if you want to leave it at we had some fun and that's it, I'm fine with that. You don't have to be an asshole about it."

Shit shit shit. I was abrupt and came off as cold and dismissive. I searched my brain for something to say to make it better but my brain and mouth refused to communicate. When a full minute of silence went by, she gave a bitter laugh.

"Fine. That's all it was. That's good. Better. I need to go explain what's happening to the rest of my pack. I'll see you around." Her body shifted. Muscles and fur rippling. The clothes she was wearing popped and tore, but mostly stayed attached. She raced through the fields towards her own camp.

"I'm sorry," I whispered. Fuck, I'd really blown that. I sighed and slipped out of my own clothes and folded them into as small a pile as I could manage. I shifted into a coyote, picked them up between my teeth, and ran back to my own camp.

When I shifted back into human form, I immediately regretted it. As a coyote I had emotions, but they were different, simpler. I didn't feel guilty or regretful like I did now.

Otter-Pup looked over the book he was reading at me. "Welcome home."

"Thanks."

"I made you a plate of food. It's the one covered in tinfoil," he said.

"You're the greatest," I said.

He grinned, stood up, and went to my tent. He returned with a black cotton dress. "Here you go."

I slipped the dress over my head, laid my clothes from last night on the table, and sat down to eat. I dug in, explaining the situation to Gemini, Juniper, and Otter-Pup. I noticed a distinct uncomfortable vibe among the pack. Gemini barely spoke, stared at their feet, nodding along. Juniper sat across from them. Smiling forcefully and responding with too much enthusiasm everything I said with, "uh huh," "wow," and "holy shit."

Otter-Pup caught my eye. He shot a glance at Gemini and then gazed at me with weighty significance. It was time I talked to Gemini, it seemed. At least it might be a good distraction to deal with someone else's feelings instead of my own.

When I finished explaining, the pack was quiet.

"So, you're saying these witches intentionally turned us into werecoyotes in hopes of controlling us with this spell. What's the end game there?" Juniper asked.

"I've been thinking about that. I don't think we're the endgame at all. We're just the test run. Foot soldiers in their creepy animal and shifter army. A bunch of punks, street kids, outsiders. There are folks who might pay attention if something like that happened to us, but I doubt it. Nobody much cared when someone turned us into werecoyotes. That's why they bought The Mechanical Anatomy and the mall above it. Build some big ritzy theater where they can turn 800 rich people at a time and they've got an army of people with all kinds of power they could use."

"Or they could be more selective and use it to blackmail people," Gemini said.

"Holy shit," Juniper said.

"Can any of you think of someone you saw in Felton that you've seen here?" I asked.

Otter-Pup's brow wrinkled. "It's a little fuzzy, but I thought I remembered seeing the lead singer of Baba Yaga and the Tricky Bitches at a show in Felton. Or someone with tattoos like that. I mean with the whole turning into a werecoyote thing, I wasn't paying a whole lot of attention to what was going on around me."

"That's what I thought, too. But, we saw the witches and none of them were in the band. Think about it for a bit. I'm starving and need to eat before I can talk or think about anything else." I locked eyes with Otter-Pup and then glanced over at Juniper. He caught the hint.

"Cool. I'm feeling motivated. June, could I beg you to help me out in the garden? I got a wicked crabgrass infestation," he said.

"Yeah, of course." She glanced at me and Gemini, stood, and the two of them wandered over to Otter-Pup's garden.

I really was hungry. I took the foil off the plate Otter-Pup left for me. Pancakes, bless him, and fruit. He hadn't gotten the fruit from the food pantry—it wasn't fresh produce day—so he must have either foraged or liberated it from the store. Whichever, I was grateful.

Gemini stood to leave.

"Let's talk," I said.

They grimaced.

"Come on. Sit down. It won't hurt, I promise."

They dropped back down on the ground and refused to make eye contact.

Anyone else and I'd give them a speech about how they didn't have to tell me anything they weren't comfortable telling me and that I was there for them when and if they ever wanted to talk. But I'd known Gemini for the better part of fifteen years and they were like a champagne bottle. They'd never open up unless someone pulled out the cork, but then there was no putting it back in: "Alright. What's up between you and Juniper? I was going to let it be since it seemed to be getting better, but now you're both being jumpy and awkward. We may live outside, but it's still close quarters and the vibe around here is getting tense. So, out with it."

Gemini sighed. "I like her."

"I know. You have for a while."

"Yeah. Well, we hooked up about a month ago."

I raised an eyebrow. That was actually a surprise, I hadn't caught wind of that. And my pack was a gossipy bunch.

"We both acted like it wasn't a big deal, but you know, I was really into her. I figured, we see each other every day, if it was going to work out, there was no need to rush it."

"Then she and Rowan got together."

They nodded and blinked a glimmer of moisture from their eyes. "Last night, she and I were alone so I decided to talk to her, tell her how I felt. She was really nice. Fuck but she was so nice about it. But, in the end, June's…"

"Straight," I finished.

They nodded. "I said she was into me enough that one night, maybe I was close enough. But she said she didn't feel that way, and even if she did, it would be too fucked up and erasing for both of us for her to treat me like a man and I shouldn't be with someone who did that."

"She's right, you know."

"Yeah, I know she's right. That's what I get, huh? Falling in love with an actual decent human for a change."

"Gemini. I'm sorry. It fucking sucks. You're a good person and Juniper is right, you deserve someone who loves and wants to fuck the brains out of the person you actually are, not the person they imagine you're close enough to being."

They laughed. "I know you're right. And if I were talking to someone else I'd say the same thing. But it's just…"

"It's just what?" I prompted.

"It just feels like… Look, June and I are both trans, right? That's a huge thing to share. And then, on top of that, there's only five of us werecoyotes. Only five people in the whole world who really get what it is to be us. And two of them are dating each other and too straight to be into a kinda butch genderfucky transwoman like me. One of them is a boy obsessed teenager. And the other one might as well be my big sister. It just feels kind of hopeless." They sighed.

"There may not be other werecoyotes, but I swear, there are other people in the world who will get you in all your weird, nerdy, prickly, brilliant, beautiful strangeness. And in the meantime, maybe no one here is fucking you, but we get you and we love you. You know that, right?"

Their eyes brimmed and they sniffled. "Goddamnit. This is why you're the pack leader, huh? You're too smart. I love you too, Mixi."

"Queer platonic, packmate, bandmate, life partners?"

"Always," they said.

I put my arm around their shoulder and held them while they frantically wiped at their eyes and I pretended that I didn't see they were crying. When they sat up, their face was puffy, but tear-free.

"Hey, so how about to distract me from my misery we talk about the raging crush you have on a werewolf."

I choked on my coffee and they grinned.

"I do not have a crush on her," I said.

They opened their eyes wide in mock surprise. "I didn't say anything about a specific werewolf. We do know six of them after all."

"Shut up."

"No seriously, you were like those goofy old ass cartoons where the dude's eyes turn into hearts and his tongue rolls out of his mouth when he sees some big-breasted lounge singer babe."

"I was not." I tossed a crumpled napkin at them.

"Aroo!" They made panting noises.

"I fucking hate you."

"Nope. You love me. You already said it. You can't take it back now."

I groaned, but smiled and nudged them in the side with my elbow. "Fine. Maybe you're right. We kissed last night."

They laughed. "Wow. Our fearless leaders. Dedicated and unfailing in their duty. So, what happened? How was it?"

"God. She's so hot and smart and funny. And then I fucked it all up. She said we should talk and I said, 'About what?' I completely and utterly blew it."

"Wow. You really, really did. But I mean, unless we all get mind fucked by witches today, you can probably fix it still."

"You think?"

They leaned against me. "No promises. R is a proud one. You're gonna have to do a lot of groveling. But yeah. I think."

CHAPTER 7

I woke from a nap to my cellphone alarm alerting me that we had a practice session scheduled at The Mechanical Anatomy in forty-five minutes. Well, shit. Rowan was still on stakeout duty, witches were still trying to turn the town into shifters so they could mind control us all, and I still felt like an asshole for hurting R's feelings. But I also still really, really wanted to win Battle of the Bands and there was only so much practicing you could do in a field with no electricity. A thousand dollars could buy a lot of hair dye and random DIY instruments for Otter-Pup. Not to mention the little blossom of egotistical hope living in my heart that thought free studio time would lead to a record deal, critical acclaim, the punk rock resurgence, and stardom.

I spotted Juniper, Otter-Pup, and Gemini sitting on the ground playing poker for lapel pins and screen-printed cotton patches. Otter-Pup appeared to be kicking their asses as he was surrounded by piles of black and white cotton and glittering buttons.

"We have practice time at The Mechanical Anatomy," I called. "Do y'all want to do it or should I call Lala to cancel?"

Gemini glanced at their diminishing pile of prized buttons and jumped to their feet. "Practice time, for sure."

Otter-Pup held up a handful of buttons to them.

"Ugh, no. You won, kid. Stop being so gracious about it," Gemini said.

Juniper laughed. "We never should have taught him how to play."

Otter-pup and I locked eyes. I smirked as he widened his eyes in mock innocence. When I met Otter-Pup, he was getting by hustling pool and cheating people at cards. As far as I knew, that was still how he got most of his spending money. He did always seem to have more cash than the rest of us. The kid could not only count cards as easy as breathing, he could read a bluff from a million miles away. But long as he wasn't cheating his bandmates out of anything but patches and buttons, I wasn't about to ruin his fun. Gemini and Juniper deserved it a little for assuming he didn't know how to play.

"I'll text Rowan and see if he needs a break. If he does, I'll go," Gemini said.

I was proud of them. It seemed like our talk helped if they were playing cards with Juniper without acting like a jerk and volunteering to talk to Rowan. Juniper smiled and looked even more relieved than I did.

While we waited for an answer from Rowan, we packed our instruments, except for Gemini, whose drums stayed in storage in a backroom of The Mechanical Anatomy. They helped Otter-Pup with his random assortment of instruments and materials.

"Rowan says to go ahead without him since we need the practice more than he does. Winky face. Smiley face. Tongue sticking out face. Guitar emoji. Heart emoji. Rainbow emoji. Dude likes his emojis," Gemini said.

Juniper grinned and her entire face lit up. God, were they in love with each other? I'd been assuming it was a fling based on proximity and mutual attraction, but we might all have to get used to them being a for-real couple. Which included the stress of a potential future break-up.

We'd deal with that later. If it happened. And if we didn't all end up as lap dogs for chicken obsessed witches.

"Alright, well let's go," I said.

We hiked back to town, weighted down by instruments slung over our backs. The sun hid behind a gauze of clouds, but the humidity was thick as peanut butter and sweat trickled between my shoulder blades. I'd need to go for a swim in the lake with half a pound of soap after practice.

When we arrived, a strain of dark, melancholy music poured from the hole leading down to the bar. I recognized the distinctive, menacing power of R's voice perfectly accented by the beauty of Ebo's electric violin. If only I could go back in time and say, 'Nah, let's skip practice today. Punk shouldn't sound *too* rehearsed.'

Gemini gave me a sideways look and whispered, "Now is as good a time as any to start on that groveling."

I sighed and we lowered our instruments down first. Then, one by one, climbed down the rope ladder after them. When I stepped inside, Lala was perched on a barstool, reading a book and tapping her foot in the air along with the music.

We set our instruments down around a rectangular, rickety table and I went to the bar.

Lala glanced up from her book and nodded. She seemed relaxed and happy, but her fingernails had been chewed down to the quick.

"How's it going?" I said.

"Not bad. I do love hosting practice for y'all. Gives me a chance to actually enjoy the music instead of trying to block it out so I can hear people's drink orders or listen for any fights I need to diffuse."

"You know, I never thought about that. I always thought it must be so cool to run a club like this. Getting to hear all the awesome bands and booking anybody you want."

"It usually is. Though sometimes I have to book some real assholes and boring ass bands who bring in money."

"I hope that's not us."

"Fuck no. Y'all don't bring in hardly any money." She winked. "But seriously, I heard some bootlegs of the Mangy Rats before you even dragged your sorry asses into town. I was excited as hell when you showed up. I'm sorry to have scheduled your practice time at the same time as Dead and Disorderly. Y'all probably shouldn't be hearing each other practice and I know they aren't your favorite people. I love them though, and this was the only time that worked for them. No offense meant."

"Shit, Lala, that's more consideration than we deserve. Besides. They're alright. You know, for the black lace and crucifix crowd."

She grinned.

"Hey, I'll let you get back to reading and enjoying the music. Thanks again, for letting us practice here." I wandered back to the band's table and pulled out a chair.

When Dead and Disorderly finished the song, Lala called out, "That's time. Wrap it up."

"Thanks," R said. She turned and gave notes and directions that we couldn't hear to the band and then they packed up and sat down at a table near the stage.

"Is it okay if we sit in for a few? Seems only fair that if you scope out our practice that we do the same." R's voice was chilly.

I glanced at Otter-Pup, Juniper, and Gemini who all shrugged.

"Yeah. Sure, it's only fair," I said through the knot in my throat.

We climbed the steps to the stage and I adjusted the microphone and tested it, then helped Otter-Pup organize his collection. Every time I glanced up, R looked away. At last I sighed. "Hey, get warmed up. I'll be right back."

I climbed back down the steps and walked towards Dead and Disorderly's table. The waves of hostility pouring off R almost made me back down. But, I noticed Ebo glance at her and roll their eyes. Maybe I had been an ass, but she was being ridiculous too. We were acting like awkward teenagers.

"Can I talk to you for a second?" I asked.

R was silent for a long, icy minute. "Fine."

She stood and I followed her to the corner of the room. Lala glanced up from her book, looked at us, and shook her head in amusement.

"I'm sorry about this morning. I was weird and abrupt and cold. That was not my intention. I was feeling a little overwhelmed and I'm not so great at talking about my own feelings," I said.

"Alright," she said.

I had no idea what to add. That was as far as I'd rehearsed.

This was when she was supposed to say, 'That's okay. I get it. Let's try making out again later.'

"Is that all?" Her voice was still harsh.

"Um."

She sighed and turned away.

"Wait. No. I am sorry. I don't know what else to say here."

R clenched her fists as if she wanted to throttle me. "I don't get what your deal is. We snipe and we have this rivalry and that's all fine. Hell, it's fun even. But now you act like you're embarrassed that you don't hate me. We can be as competitive as you want. So do you like me or do you hate me? Pick."

Was I embarrassed that I was into her? Maybe that was true. We'd been rivals since she got to town. That wasn't it, though. Not entirely. Maybe I'd felt that way at first but, I wasn't embarrassed that I liked *her*, I was uncomfortable having feelings for *anyone*. There'd been one-night stands, but I hadn't really been involved with anyone in four years. Not since becoming a werecoyote. Even though I should know she'd understand that, I couldn't find the words to explain it. She shook her head and started to walk away.

"Wait. Hey, um everybody," I said.

My bandmates stopped pretending to fiddle with their instruments while they watched us from the corners of their eyes and R's bandmates continued to gaze at us with unabashed amusement.

"I like R. I mean, I *like* her. A lot."

"Wow. I'm shocked. I had no idea," Juniper said drily.

"Complete surprise to me too," Gemini said.

"Are you going to kiss each other again?" Otter-Pup's face split in a wicked grin.

From R's table, Ebo chimed in. "I think I speak for everyone when I say, duh. That's been obvious since we came to town."

"Everybody knows," Lala shouted from the back.

I pressed my hand to my forehead and laughed. R paused and looked back at me, also laughing and blushing.

"See? No embarrassment. I mean, except for the fact that I'm apparently about as subtle as a horny tomcat," I said.

She gazed at me for a long moment, a smirk curling the

corners of her lips.

"Is there anything I can do to make it up to you?"

Her voice dropped so only I could hear her. "I'll certainly think of something." She walked away, a graceful swish in her hips made my cheeks warm and tied my tongue in knots.

When I recovered my senses, I climbed back onto the stage. Gemini counted us off and we ran through our set. It sounded weak without Rowan and his bass. At the end of each song we paused and gave each other feedback. Though no one ever really knew what to say to Otter-Pup. We just let him do his thing. It was ninety-five percent improvisation and, except for a few lyric queues, he did something different every single time no matter what I said.

The door screeched open and heavy, drunken sounding footsteps started down the ramp.

"Help, we need help," Rowan's strangled voice called from the entryway.

CHAPTER 8

R beat me to the entrance and her face paled. She reached up and Rowan lowered KC into her arms. "God, what happened?"

"The witches. They knew we were there," Rowan said, his voice pained and tearful.

Otter-Pup stood beside me and gripped my arm tight. Tears welled in his eyes and his mouth opened and closed in horror.

Lala stood, stern and business-like. "Lay him out on the table."

R carried him easily and laid him gently on the table top. His olive skin was shot through with red spider webs and sweat soaked his long hair.

Juniper went to Rowan's side and touched his arm. "You're burning up."

"You sit down." Lala pointed at Rowan who followed her command.

Lala leaned over KC and pried open his eyes. His pupils and irises were entirely obscured by a thick blood red film. She opened his mouth to reveal bloody gums and ugly white sores.

She looked up at me and R. "He's been hexed. You know anything about it?"

The words spilled out of R's mouth fast and clumsy like

marbles from a bag. She told her everything. As R spoke, Lala's eyes went wider.

"You're saying witches bought my bar so they could turn a bunch of rich people into shifters that they can control."

"Do you know something?" I asked.

She glanced at me with a weak smile. "We all have our pasts. Gemini, I need you to get me a bag. It's in the room next to where I let you store your drums. It's bright red, you can't miss it." She handed them a key.

They took it and ran through the bar and disappeared backstage. They returned carrying a crimson bag with bone handles etched with beautiful symbols. She took the bag from Gemini, squeezed the handles for several seconds until they hummed and opened with a snap. Tiny drops of blood appeared on Lala's palm where she had gripped it.

She noticed me staring. "Security. Also ensures I don't open it unless I'm serious." Lala took out bottles and started mixing liquids. Purple, red, black, and something that pale yellow with lumps in it that looked horribly like the clumps of fat that clung to a steak.

"You're a witch. I mean, I knew you practiced. But, like a real witch," Juniper said.

Lala began to chant and sing. It was beautiful. I couldn't understand the words, but they rose and turned sharp like daggers and then fell into lush, pillow-like softness. I remembered the description of the spell I'd found. It involved tone, rhythm, music—I glanced at R, but she looked terrified, eyes fixed on KC. I squeezed her hand and she clung to mine so tight it hurt. Between her on one side and Otter-Pup on the other, my hands were starting to ache, but I didn't complain.

Lala stopped singing and filled a shot glass with the repulsive liquid, pouring the rest into a whiskey glass. She handed the shot glass to Rowan. "You've got it too, drink it down fast, it's going to taste horrid. Whatever you do, don't throw it back up or you'll regret it. A lot."

Rowan looked at the shot glass apprehensively.

"You're a punk, Rowan. You've taken shots of liquor that could disintegrate steel. You got this," I said.

He gave me a shaky smile, took a deep breath, and poured the shot down his throat. He gagged and Juniper clapped a hand over his mouth. He swallowed and sat down, his face pale and sweaty, but the alarming red spiderwebs around his eyes shrank and paled.

Lala turned back to KC. "This is going to be harder. Can one of you hold him up in a sitting position, but keep his head tilted back?"

Both R and Otter-Pup released my hands simultaneously and stepped forward. R pulled KC up on the table and leaned him against her while Otter-Pup held his head in place.

With a dropper, Lala dripped the liquid in his throat, bit by bit. When the glass was empty but for a yellow, slimy sheen, she stepped back.

"Well?" R asked.

"That's all I can do for now."

"Is he going to be okay?" Otter-Pup asked.

"I don't know. The hex that they put on the two of them was a nasty one. It's like a vicious, fast acting blood infection. They must have targeted KC, but you can make a hex reverberate. Just like when you hit a cymbal. A sharp impact on the target and then waves pour out from them for a few seconds and hit anyone nearby. In this case, KC was the cymbal. If Rowan'd been closer to KC when it hit, they'd probably both be in this condition."

"And therefore dead," R finished.

"Yeah," Lala agreed. "If he pulls through, it won't be today. He'll be unconscious for a couple of days at least."

"Fuck." R leaned down and stroked KC's hand. "You gotta be alright. We need you to keep us out of trouble."

I glanced at Rowan. Guilty as it made me feel, I was glad it wasn't him who had been the target. I could only imagine how hurt and scared R was right now. Exactly how I'd feel if it had been one of my pack.

"They have to pay for this," Maezi said.

"They will," R said.

"Lala, do you have any idea who it might be behind this? We think it must be a musician. They worked the spell to turn us when we were performing or watching shows in different bars

62

around the country, they might have played here. Maybe you felt them."

She tapped her fingers on the table. "I wish I knew. For KC's sake and my own. If some witches are trying to hurt people using my bar, I want to know about it. But, there are a lot of witches who play here, just like there are a lot of shifters. I couldn't begin to guess. But I haven't sensed any spellwork from the stage apart from some minor glamors. Maybe they haven't played here yet. After all, you all are still here, full of free will."

"We have seen them. But not here." I described the four people we'd seen outside.

Something flashed across Lala's face and disappeared. "I've never seen anyone who looked like that in here. But if they're witches, it's likely they're using a glamor to change their appearances."

"Shit. Of course, they are. Even I could do that one as a kid," I said.

Lala shot me an exhausted smile. "That is the first spell most young witch wannabes try their hand at. Getting your first pimples is a real bitch. Let's get KC as comfortable as we can. I've got a cot in back."

I moved to help, but R shook her head gently at me. She and her pack carefully lifted KC and followed Lala backstage.

"You too, Rowan. You need to rest and let the spell clear all the poison out of your system. Let's go." Lala gestured.

He grimaced, but followed without protest.

Otter-Pup plopped down in a chair and put his chin in his hands, looking miserable.

"What are we gonna do?" Juniper asked.

"We're going back." R stepped onto the stage.

"To the witches' house?" I asked.

She nodded. "For KC and Rowan."

I stood and pulled out a chair. "Okay. But we're not going in without a plan."

She nodded and sat down.

Maezi, Ebo, and Bee came out and joined us.

"Cole wants to stay with KC," Ebo said.

R nodded. "We're coming up with a plan to go after the

witches."

Bee nodded solemnly.

"Good," Maezi said.

"What plan do we need besides go in and kick ass?" Gemini frowned.

"Don't go back there." Lala stood silently, watching us from the doorway leading backstage.

"Why?" I asked.

"They're dangerous."

"We started this to help you," I said.

"Who asked you to do that?" she snapped. Her face softened. "I'm sorry, Mixi. Look, I've known witches like them. Most of us are decent folk, but like everybody, some of us are incredibly shitty people. And when witches are shitty people we can do all kinds of damage."

"Lala, do you know them?" R asked.

She shrugged. "How could I know that? I just know that they're willing to do some dark magic. Some very dark magic. You know what the cost is for a spell like that? A darkening of the spellcaster's soul. When they die, their soul is stuck on earth forever. And it would have needed *at least* two quarts of blood from a person whose blood has never been used for a spell before. That means they didn't get it from themselves and I doubt anyone volunteered. These witches are willing to destroy themselves and innocent people just to hurt or kill someone who caught on to their plans. I can't even imagine what the cost could be for the spell they're planning."

"So, what? We let them keep going? If we don't try and stop them, it sounds like they're going to hurt or kill a lot of people. This is bigger than just saving The Mechanical Anatomy," I said.

"Lala, if there's anything you can do to help, we welcome it. But we're doing this. With or without you," R said.

Lala buried her face in her hands and groaned. "Fuck. Alright, let me see the pages you stole."

I handed the crumpled papers over. Lala nibbled at the remains of her thumbnail as she read. A strange look crossed her face. A kind of terrified resignation. At last she set the pages on the table in front of her. "You're right about the spell being woven into music. And the image in blood means tattoos."

"How do you know that?" R asked.

She smiled sadly. "Call it a hunch. I mean, it could be a painting done in blood, but it's tattoos. A sacrifice of blood and pain from the spellcaster in addition to whatever other ingredients are required."

"The Tricky Bitches. We were right about seeing them in Felton, but dismissed them without considering glamors," I said. "But that fucking chicken tattoo on her chest."

Lala jumped as if electrocuted.

"Alright, Lala. Something's up. Are you going to tell us or let us go in without knowing everything?" R asked.

"I just didn't consider it was someone I booked here. I mean, they shouldn't have been able to sneak past me with that much dark on their souls," she said.

Lala was lying, I was certain of that. But, I couldn't force it out of her. I just had to hope she was telling us everything that might be important.

"If you insist on doing this, let me give you some protection." Lala stood up from the table.

"That would be great, thanks," R said.

When she was gone, R leaned across the table. "What the hell?"

"She knows something she's not saying," Bee said.

"Do we need to be worried, do you think?" Gemini asked.

"I don't think so. You saw her bag? She said she had to be serious about using it if she opened it. I think Lala got in deep with some dark magic and ran away from some scary ass witches," I said.

"That would make sense. Alright. Well, I say we can't trust her completely, but I'm not real worried she's trying to get us hurt," R said.

"That's a good assessment," I agreed.

She leaned back as Lala returned with five skulls that looked like birds. She set them on the table. "I'm sorry, I only have five."

I picked one up and fingered it lightly. "What are they?"

"Banshee skulls," she said.

"Excuse me?" I set it back down gingerly.

She smiled. "They can't keep away everything, but a living banshee screams because she senses death coming. Her skull still senses death so combined with the right magic, can deflect things that have the potential to kill. They won't do anything against spells that make you itch, ache, get confused, lock up your muscles, and even a few very specific spells that can dismember bloodlessly. But at least you should be hard to kill."

"Thanks, Lala. That means five people are going. Everybody else can wait outside and prepare to help with a hasty escape if need be," R said.

I exchanged glances with the werecoyotes and they all nodded. "Agreed. I'm going for sure," I said.

"Me too. We'll do this the coyote way. Volunteers only," R said.

Everyone either raised their hands.

My heart swelled. Shifters, punks, goths, and queers. The bravest and biggest hearts in the fucking world.

"Alright. Well, I'm going to say Gemini because they're a master with a lock pick and we might need that," I said.

"And I say Bee because she has the most experience with witchcraft of all the wolves," R said.

That was four. Who should be the fifth?

Otter-Pup raised his hand and my heart sank. I loved every one of the coyotes like family, but no one punched my protective buttons like Otter-Pup.

His hands fluttered nervously at his sides, but there was a steel determination in his face. "I want to go. I know all the wolves love KC in a way no one else can. But, he's important to me, too. And Rowan bought me my first binder and showed me how to tie a tie when I went to my dad's funeral. He's like the big brother I never got to have. I'm little and not the best fighter or good at picking locks or knowledgeable about witchcraft, but I can talk myself out of any situation and I can memorize anything I see in seconds. If we get caught, or find more books we need to study, that might be more important than who has the biggest teeth."

I looked at R willing her to give me a reason to say 'no.' By rights, KC was the one near death, the fifth person should be a wolf, but she was the one who would have to make that claim.

But instead she smiled at Otter-Pup. "I'd be more than happy to have you at my back."

He swelled with pride. God help me, but I wasn't going to argue.

"That's it then. Let's go," I said.

We each picked up our banshee skull and hung it around our necks on silk chains. Mine dropped beneath my shirt. It felt as warm as living flesh against my skin and I shuddered.

CHAPTER 9

We arrived at the witches' house and, apart from the clucking of chickens, it was silent. R gave me a tight-lipped smile. We were really about to do this. Storm the gates to the house of the wicked witches. I took a deep breath and slipped through the hole in the fence. Heat tickled my skin and the banshee skull around my neck moved, jerking against the chain, and let out a soft moan. I froze. I should have asked more questions about how Lala's charms worked.

Before anyone else could follow me through I held a hand up against the steel mesh. "The skull moved when I climbed through."

R turned to Bee, who nodded. "They must have found the hole and put a spell on it. Good thing we have these or you'd be dead."

My heart drummed and my mouth dried at the thought of my near miss. "Should you all find a different way through? Just in case."

Otter-Pup stood straight and tall as he could. "We don't have time. The skull protected you. It will do the same for us."

"He's right. We should also assume that they know we're coming now," Bee said.

Gemini bunched their hands and dove through the hole, the

fence rattled around them. They stood and breathed a sigh of relief. "It tickled, but I'm alright."

One by one, they all followed. Bee reacted the strongest, her face twisting in discomfort, and she rubbed her arms when she got to the other side. Maybe because she was the most sensitive to magic.

As we got closer to the house, the chickens drew closer until we were surrounded by a net of feathers and clucking. I spotted the glowing, green eyed terror at the front, directly in front of us. I linked arms with Gemini and Otter-Pup and saw R and Bee do the same. We moved as a unit towards the back door where the wolves had gotten in without trouble last time, but the chickens moved with us, their circle slowly tightening .

"They can't kill us," R whispered.

"No but they can hurt us," Bee said.

"I say we make a run for it," Gemini said.

"Are we wolves and coyotes, or aren't we? Chickens fear us, not the other way around," R said. She dropped to all fours and shifted. Black and silver fur rippled down her muscular body and she snapped at the chickens. Bee followed suit, her black and purple locs disappearing under soft gray fur. They looked hilarious with their clothes, shredded, stretched, and hanging from their wolf bodies. Like werewolves in an old black and white movie.

I looked at Gemini and Otter-Pup and shrugged. "Hopefully no one goes full wolf and remembers wolves and coyotes hate each other." My vision turned sharp, colors faded to grays and blacks, and my ears elongated. When I dropped to my hands and knees, the chickens started to smell appetizing.

The wolf smell raised my hackles, but I retained enough of myself to remember they weren't my enemies, and the comforting presence of my pack at my side calmed me. We raced, snapping, and barking through the mess of chickens. R reached the porch first and shifted gracefully back into herself. Not bothering with subtly this time, she wrapped the remains of her jacket around her arm, smashed the window on the door, reached through, and unlocked it. We bolted inside after her and she shut the door. We all returned to our human shapes, clothes torn and hanging. My black jeans were gone, torn and kicked off when they prevented me from running, so I was left in black boxer briefs and a shredded t-shirt. I was glad I'd worn briefs today, at least they provided some cover.

R gave my butt a quick appreciate glance. She blushed when I caught her eye and winked.

"Well, definitely no one is home. They'd have heard that racket if they were," Gemini said.

"So much for storming the castle to defeat the witch. What do we do? Lay in wait for them to come back?" Bee asked.

"I guess. We should look around. See if there's anything we missed last time. Someone should watch both doors though," R said.

"Ideally no one should be alone, but we have an odd number. How about Gemini watches the front door, Bee watches the back. Otter-Pup, do a back and forth patrol to keep an eye on both. R and I will look around. Everyone agree?" I asked.

Nods all around as everyone spread out to their positions.

A loud caw startled me and I turned to see a crow hop through the window R had broken. It flapped to the ground and hopped back and forth on it's yellow-orange feet, its wings spread wide and dipping side to side in an odd dance.

"What the fuck? Is this another of the witches' mind-control birds?" R asked.

It hopped in front of me and I tensed. It held something shiny in its talons. It dropped the object and hopped away from me. I looked down to see a flattened neon pink bottle cap. I gingerly picked it up and flipped it over. It said Oak Tree Brews. A shitty, weak, raspberry flavored pale ale that he bought anytime he came into enough money. I smiled.

R tilted her head and gave me a quizzical look.

I held it up. "It's Otter-Pup's favorite. I'm not sure, but I think the bird came from Lala."

The crow cawed and hopped down the hall toward the room Gemini had searched when we were last here. It pecked at the closed door. R opened it and a wave of heat and the putrid stench of rot poured out. I gagged, but followed the crow inside.

Either Gemini had severely understated what they found, or

the witches had been busy. Almost every surface had been draped with bloody pelts. I shifted enough that my nose elongated into a stubby snout. The distinctive musk of coyote tickled my nose followed by wolf. There reeked of chickens, same as every other inch of the house, but also fox, and something with scales that I didn't recognize.

I shifted my face back and turned to R. Her own nose was long, black, and wet as she sniffed the air as well. From the hard, dark gleam in her eyes, she must have smelled the same things I had.

The crow hopped through the room, hesitant and wary now. Probably as frightened by the smell of death as much as we were. It stopped and did a strange, open winged dance. R walked closer and it hopped away from her, but didn't leave. She stood where it had been dancing and they watched each other. When R didn't move, it hopped back, only inches from her feet and began its strange dance again. Then it hopped back and watched her.

R knelt and ran her hands over the floor. Despite all the blood and death, the tan carpet was clean. She dug her fingers between the carpet and the wall and lifted it easily from the floor. The unfinished wood underneath was peeling from water damage and stained with blood.

Exactly beneath where the crow had been dancing was a round, rusting handle. R looked up at me. I nodded and crouched, ready to attack whatever, or whoever, might come out.

She gripped the handle and lifted, her muscles straining. A large section of the floor rose and as soon as the door stood at a ninety-degree angle, she shoved it over. It fell open with a heavy thud.

The crow cawed once and took off, flying out of the room, and I assumed, out of the house. Smart fucking bird.

Whatever lay below was dark, so R and I both shifted our entire heads giving us access to all our canid senses. She was still beautiful. Like an ancient forest goddess someone might paint on the side of a vase or a temple. I shook my now heavy head. We were about to jump into who knows what and I was mooning over a babe with a wolf head.

I held her legs as she lowered herself down for a better look. She gasped and I immediately yanked her back out.

Her face shifted back to human. "There's someone down there. I couldn't see their faces, but they aren't moving. I don't think they're dead though." She shifted her head back to the wolf and without any warning, jumped straight into the cellar.

Shit shit shit. I couldn't let her go alone. I jumped after her. I bent my knees to absorb some of the impact, but the landing still sent shudders through my bones.

Three people sat in metal folding chairs. They sat so still that I might have thought they were statues if I couldn't smell them. None of them glanced at us, blinked, or showed any sign they knew we were there.

I recognized them. It was the Tricky Bitches. Everyone except the lead singer. The one in the center's eyes suddenly lit up and glowed pale green. They turned their heads to the side in perfect unison and stared at us as feathers sprouted along their arms and cheeks.

"Holy shit," R murmured. She had shifted her face back to human. I was hesitant to follow suit, not wanting to lose my night vision.

The one with green eyes threw herself at R while the other two leapt at me. The banshee skulls around our necks twitched and jerked and howled. All three of the bewitched people leapt back as if they'd touched something hot. The skull grew heavier and warmer, feeling more fleshy and alive against my skin. Every time one of them started to race towards us, the skulls shrieked and they fell back further.

I allowed my face to return to human. "They can't hurt us, thank you Lala, and since they're cursed, it doesn't feel right to hurt them. I'll keep an eye on them while you look around."

R nodded and shifted her face back into the huge, silky wolf head. She sniffed the air and disappeared behind me. The three went utterly still once again, only their eyes moving, flicking back and forth as they watched R search.

She returned to my side with a well worn journal in her hands. She flipped through the pages. "I found a bunch of spell books, but also look." She pointed at a hand drawn map with red dots in several cities. Including Felton and Oak Tree Harbor.

"All places they've been I bet," I said.

"And this journal is full of the results of magical experiments. Read this one."

I took the journal gingerly, as if afraid just touching it could activate the spells inside. "Experiment a success. Subjects transformed into chickens both on command and during the standard full moon. Able to maintain control over them in both human and bird form."

"Of course they made werechickens. What else. They really love chickens," I said.

"Or hate them, maybe."

I handed the journal back to her. "I still feel like we're missing something. What exactly do we do with it? I mean, is it enough to prove they used witchcraft to buy The Mechanical Anatomy?"

R hesitated and sighed. "I did find a bill of sale back there. It looks legit."

The cellar door slammed shut and I jumped.

CHAPTER 10

The light flicked on. After being in darkness, we were momentarily blinded. When my eyes adjusted, a woman stood before us. It was the lead singer of the Tricky Bitches. Baba Yaga, I guess. A little on the nose. On either side of her neck, the skin was raised and pink around fresh tattoos. On one side of her neck was a face that was wolf on one side and a girl wearing the skin of a wolf as a hood on the other. The other side of her neck was a mirror, but depicting a coyote in place of the wolf. The coyote tattoo was kind of shitty, as if the artist just drew a wolf and narrowed its face. I was a little insulted.

She glared at her three stone-faced bandmates. The one with glowing green eyes flinched, but the other two were unfazed. I remembered that book I'd stolen pages from; didn't it say that the witch only really held the will of one animal while the others in range of the spell were like living zombies?

The witch pointed at me and snapped her fingers, hissing words I couldn't understand. The banshee skull around my neck pulsed wildly and swung back and forth as magic tickled my skin. The tickling intensified as the witch's face twisted into a snarl and her chanting grew louder. The cellar was basically a large, concrete box and the ear splitting banshee shriek echoed horribly.

Her eyes widened. "Now, where would a bunch of shifters get

74

banshee skulls?"

R's eyes locked on the witch and her muscles tensed. R was about to rush her. I decided I'd let her go first, bowl the witch over. Then I'd shift and follow-up with teeth and claws.

But the witch laughed. "Maybe I can't kill you, my little coyote. But, I can do other things."

She snapped her fingers and I was on my back. My head bounced on the concrete and my legs locked, like all the bones had been replaced with steel beams.

R froze. "Mixi. Are you alright?"

"Oh, they're fine. Not dead. But they left a little something behind for me. A gift on my sister's beak."

"A gift—oh god, the fucking chicken," I said. "Wait, your *sister*?"

"Hm. Yes. One of them. Family can be so troublesome, don't you think?" She snapped her fingers and my body rose and flipped until she dropped me on my stomach. The leaden feeling in my legs spread to my hips and then to the muscles in my back until I was gasping for air, suffocating under the weight of my own bones.

"Let Mixi go," R demanded.

"Certainly. Take off the banshee skull, wolf."

R shook her head.

"Very well. I can do this forever. So long as I have no intention to kill the little coyote, the banshee skulls can do nothing."

She snapped her fingers and the heaviness spread to my skull. Everything ached. It felt as though I'd collapse under myself, shattering into a thousand pieces, and yet, I just got heavier and heavier. The bones in my wrists protruded from my skin, stretching further and further until they glowed faint white through flesh as thin as paper. It was almost beautiful.

"Fine," R said.

"No." I groaned as the bones in my back popped and tore at my clothes. Was I growing *spines*?

"I'm sorry, what was that?" The witch snapped her fingers again and my bones shifted and grew so heavy that the concrete cracked underneath my body and something hard and boney popped through the skin of my fingertips.

I screamed. Seeing my own bones in the open air, now curved and hooked, was nightmarish. But it didn't bleed. Not a drop of blood fell from the wound.

"I'll take it off. Just don't hurt them," R said, her voice soft and defeated.

The witch muttered a few words and my bones contracted again. It was agonizing. But then it was over. My body ached, but I was fine. I sat up, air flowing through my lungs, easy and delicious.

R stood face to face with the witch. She held her head in defiance as the witch raised one hand and began to sing. Her voice was beautiful. Hypnotic. I forgot what I was doing and swayed side to side.

I remembered that voice. I remembered this feeling. Like running through the open fields, stars like rivers of fireflies lighting the way above me. It sounded like curling up, warm and furry with my pack. It was wild and it was home.

As the song grew louder, R dropped to her knees and her eyes glowed like emeralds.

Fear shot through me like a slap of ice cold water in the face. This witch was taking R from me. R was home, too.

Binding magic… an image drawn in blood.

I ran towards her. Even though my bones ached and protested, I shifted, gray and golden-brown fur sprouting from my hands. My fingers shortened, the nails disappeared inside, and claws blossomed. I swiped at the side of the witch's neck and aimed for the wolf girl.

My claws slid through her flesh like she was any other beast. The tattoo shredded and bled. She screamed and started to work her magic on me again, but it was too late. R was free of her spell, fully in wolf form, and only a foot away from her.

R's lips curled and she snarled. The witch jumped backwards, but R's teeth raked the other side of her neck, tearing up the shitty coyote tattoo, along with a large chunk of the witch's throat. Bleeding and wobbling, the witch fell, panting to the ground. She raised her arms in front of her face. A plea for mercy, surrender.

R froze. Rigid, hackles raised, and blood dripping from her

muzzle. I didn't know what she'd do. I wasn't sure how much of R was present and how much was pure wolf.

Slowly, the wolf shifted back into the woman. R stood, her eyes bright with rage and blood smeared across her face. With one hand still furry and clawed, she swiped at the witch's chest and tore up the chicken tattoo.

The three members of the Tricky Bitches started screaming like banshees.

CHAPTER 11

It took several minutes to get the bewitched musicians to calm down. Understandable. I'd be in a panic too if I suddenly returned to my own mind and realized that not only was I a werechicken, but that I'd had my entire life hijacked by a witch for at least four years. Their names turned out to be Nettle, Fi, and PJ.

Footsteps pounded on the floor upstairs. Probably Gemini, Otter-Pup, and Bee. R and I shoved the heavy cellar door back open while Nettle, Fi, and PJ kept angry, careful watch over the witch.

I poked my head out through the cellar door and saw Gemini.

"Oh, thank fuck," they said when they saw me.

"We got the witch. We also found the Tricky Bitches. Turns out they've been under a curse this whole time. Could you grab the others and help us get everyone out? The witch is pretty bloodied up, the Tricky Bitches are weak from being chickens and trapped in a cellar, and the witch whammied me pretty hard."

Gemini nodded and ran to grab Bee and Otter-Pup. We got the Tricky Bitches out first and Otter-Pup took them out of the room to get sunlight, air, water, and any food they trusted not be hexed. Then I grabbed Gemini's hand and climbed out.

"You can leave, now. Thank you for your help," a warm,

earthy voice said.

A woman with brown skin and curly black hair stood in the doorway. She was dressed like a woman who'd walked out of an old photo of an old west school marm. Except she was clad completely in the most lush crimson. Her dress buttoned at the throat and wrists with onyx buttons and the lace hem brushed the ground.

"Excuse me?" Bee said.

"We'll deal with our sister." Another woman appeared behind the first. She was a pale, icy blonde dressed almost identically but in soothing, velvety cobalt. Something about her was familiar: the tilt of her head, the sharp edges of her nose.

"You're that chicken," I whispered.

She smiled. "I am sorry about that. But I was quite literally not myself at the time."

The witch down in the cellar with R screamed. "No. You can't leave me with them. You think I'm bad? You have no idea."

"Hush." R hopped up, pulling herself out of the cellar. "Why should we trust you to take care of her?"

"What are you going to do?" the former chicken asked. "Turn her in to the police? Jeza is very talented. She'll convince them you're insane at best, the actual kidnappers at worst. Or she'll melt everyone's bones and walk out the door."

"Or you could just execute her now. We won't stop you," the one in red said coolly.

"How do we know you didn't have a part in her plan?" Otter-Pup asked.

The blonde wrinkled her nose. "Jeza had a fascination with shifters and animal magic that we permitted but did not share. Ask your friend Lala if you can trust us."

Gemini and I exchanged looks. "You know Lala?" I asked.

"Our sister," they said in unison.

"Though she refuses to have anything to do with us anymore," one added sadly.

Fuck. That was a big thing Lala had been hiding.

R nodded to Bee who pulled her phone from her pocket and dialed.

"Hey Lala. So, we have three witches here. One is named Jeza and the other two, who have chosen to remain nameless, say they're your sisters. They want to, and I quote, deal with Jeza for us and insist they had nothing to do with the plot against you and the plot to turn everyone into mindless shifter minions. Should we trust them and let them take her?"

Bee nodded as she listed. "Um, well they were both mind-fucked, vicious yard chickens at the time." She was quiet again as she listened. "Got it. No, it's cool. You're Lala. You should have told us, though. We would have understood. Bye."

"Lala says that under no circumstance should we trust the two of them. But that they're lawful evil types who'd never have any part in animal magic. Also, we probably can rely on them to deal with Jeza given how pissed they must be at her," Bee said.

"Good enough for me. Mixi?" R said.

I shrugged. "I can't say I like it. But don't see another choice. You two going to leave Lala and The Mechanical Anatomy alone?"

They both nodded.

"We would like Lala to return. There should always be three. But, we'll find another. And I don't even know what a Mechanical Anatomy is," the former chicken said.

"Then, I guess I'm fine with it, too. But, we'll be back if you don't live up to your end." I did my best to look stern and commanding.

The two witches smiled so I must not have achieved the desired effect. But I was happy to have Jeza off my hands. Besides, something about these two suggested that whatever I decided, they were going to do what they wanted anyway. There was a power there I didn't want to mess with. I was quite sure that I'd used up whatever luck I had for a while.

CHAPTER 12

R slipped her fingers into the belt loops of my black jeans and pulled me against her. I rested my hands against the small of her back and pressed into her warm, soft body as tightly as I could. She dipped her head down to kiss me and I inhaled the smell of her. Sweat, pine trees, and soap.

I slipped my hand under her shirt and traced my fingernails down her back. She arched against me and kissed me deeper. I loved this part. Those moments with a new lover where you found out that nibbling their earlobe was a ticklish spot that made them giggle or that a quick flick of tongue across a nipple made them moan. Everything about her was intoxicating. I could stay here forever.

Someone knocked on the door and I groaned.

"Go away," R yelled, teasing.

"Come on, we have a show to play," Gemini shouted.

"I guess we do," I said.

R ran her hands over my mohawk and secured a strand that always liked to droop into my eyes.

I gave her a quick, firm kiss. "You know, after everything that's happened, this whole battle of the bands thing…"

"Seems really fucking important?"

I laughed. "Damn right it does. We are so going to kick your asses. Your sexy, lace covered asses." My hand slid down the back of her tight black pants.

"In your dreams."

She slipped an arm around my waist as we walked towards the stage. I squeezed her hand once and joined my pack while she joined hers to watch as Lala opened the show.

The stage lights were bright and the bar was packed. Lala stepped up to the mic and cleared her throat. "Many of you have heard, but tonight is going to be the last ever Battle of the Bands at The Mechanical Anatomy."

A groan went up over the crowd.

"I know. Thanks to the help of some very dear friends—" she turned and smiled at us, "—we were saved from being sold just to be demolished and turned into a theater, but nothing could save us from health and public safety inspectors."

"Fascists," someone yelled from the crowd.

Otter-Pup gripped my hand, his eyes wide and his face sad.

I squeezed him back. "We'll be okay. Lala will be okay, too. I promise."

"But, if it has to end, I'm glad it's ending with these two bands, which are without a doubt, two of the greatest bands ever to grace this shit town. So, make sure to cast your vote in the back using the very high tech, fifteen-year-old computer I dug up from an old storage room, and put your hands together for the Mangy Rats."

The bar erupted in cheers and hoots as we ran out on the stage.

If nothing else, our last show at The Mechanical Anatomy was a good one. My vocals were powerful and filled with a vibrant, rich rage I was cultivating over the loss of one of the best venues I'd ever played. Otter-Pup bounced and slammed his new sledgehammer against sheet metal and whipped it back and forth until it sounded like thunder, blew on a kazoo at just the right moment to mock the consumer frenzy of the rich folks in Hammond, and beat a trash can lid with a brick until the brick broke apart into chunks of red rock and he started handing out the pieces to people screaming in delight in the front row. Gemini raged on their drums like some kind tireless god. Juniper played her guitar to the frantic joy of the room as if she hated the fucking thing, and Rowan's majestic bass added an air of dark menace to the set.

Basically, we were fucking amazing.

Then our time was up and the crowd cheered and stomped. I grinned at Gemini. There was no way we were going to lose.

Then Dead and Disorderly stepped on stage. And shit, but they were good. I'd known they were good, but I let our rivalry cloud just how good they really were. R was a master songwriter. Her lyrics were a perfect match to her throaty, dark, low voice. She swayed and danced, jumping and shouting with their harder songs, mesmerizing the audience like a praying mantis preparing to bite off her prey's head during the slow ones. Beautiful and threatening and sexy as hell. The crowd was quieter while they played, but only because they were completely enraptured by her.

When they were done, Lala gave everyone fifteen minutes to drink and vote. My band and I joined Dead and Disorderly backstage.

"You were amazing," I said, trying to not sound begrudging but fairly certain I failed.

R kissed my cheek. "So were you. Fuck, I don't think I've ever seen you all so in sync before. It was incredible to watch."

With a shock, I recognized my own feelings in her voice. Just like me, she knew her band was good, but was desperate to be the best, and thought she was going to lose tonight. That realization didn't mean I didn't care who won or lost. I cared. I cared a lot.

Lala flashed the lights and the crowd silenced. She climbed the steps to the stage and lowered the microphone. "Ladies, gentlequeers, and dudes. It was very close, but we have a winner."

The room was utterly silent for what felt like forever.

"Put your hands together for the winner of the final Battle of the Bands. Dead and Disorderly."

My heart sank and my body felt like a deflated balloon as the crowd burst into cheers. A few people booed.

R and her pack cheered and hugged one another and practically danced out on the stage.

"Well, shit. I'd say, next time. But if there's a next time, it'll have to be somewhere else, huh?" Gemini said.

I nodded, not quite able to speak through my disappointment.

R took the check and the letter giving them free studio time from Lala and held them high while her band clapped each other on the back. Then she stepped up to the mic and though it killed me a little, seeing the grin on her gorgeous face made me feel a little better about our loss.

"Thank you everybody. We are so fucking honored." She cleared her throat and glanced over at Lala. "But, there's been a change of plans."

The crowd murmured in confusion and Lala frowned.

"Will the Mangy Rats join me on stage?"

I stood straight up and my pack shot confused glances at me.

I shrugged. "I have no idea what she's doing."

Otter-Pup hopped out onto the stage to a large round of applause and the rest of us followed.

R beckoned me over and grabbed my hand. A few people whistled and hooted cheerfully. She squeezed my hand tight and I realized she was nervous, so I squeezed her back.

"The Mechanical Anatomy is *not* a lost cause!" R said into the mic. "Lala still owns this place, she just needs to get it fixed up. Fuck, this place doesn't even have a backdoor if someone needs to bolt if a cop in. It can be even better than it is."

"I don't have that kind of money–" Lala started.

R held up her hand. "Tonight is no longer Battle of the Bands. Tonight is a benefit concert to save The Mechanical Anatomy. So, get out your wallets and call any friends or family you have who aren't here right now for some reason and tell them to get their asses over to The Mechanical Anatomy. Especially if any of your friends and family are rich or work construction and want to donate some free labor."

The crowd laughed.

"I don't even care if they live in town. They got time, because the two best bands in Oak Tree Harbor are going to be playing here, all fucking night."

The crowd roared.

"To show you how serious I am about this," she turned around, "Lala, here is your check back. I'm donating it. Use it to save this place."

Lala's hands were tentative as she reached out and took the check. "You sure about this?"

"Completely," she said.

"Join us on stage for a number?" R asked me.

I grinned. "Absolutely."

Rowan and Juniper grabbed their guitars, Gemini joined Maezi on the drums, and R and I stood side-by-side as the music rose around us.

Fuck. I was definitely in love with a werewolf.

Acknowledgments

Lots of people went into the making of this the book and into the care and feeding of the author during the writing, submitting, and publishing phases.

First, dave ring, publisher and editor extraordinaire. Julia Rios, who was the first one to see promise in these disaster queers. The *Ashes* collective, Meg Elison, Premee Mohamed, Tlotlo Tsamaase, and Sabrina Vourvoulias, who always made sure I knew I wasn't alone. Merc Fenn Wolfmoor, who patiently listened to my screams of joy and frustration from start to finish. Elsa Sjunneson, who quite honestly kept me going as a writer when the shit hit the fan. Nibedita Sen and Nino Cipri, who were there to celebrate with me when things finally went right.

Thanks to everyone both online and in the pub who gave me support and shouted their enthusiasm. Without you, this book most definitely wouldn't have made it into the world.

Thanks to my mom for teaching me to love libraries and my dad for taking me to the bookstore to buy me books and giant chocolate chip cookies when my mom worked nights. Mama Rostholder, who is probably my biggest fan. Libby Grahn, the best friend a queer could ask for, I look forward to growing older and queerer alongside you! Even (especially?) my fur beasts: Anya, Hoa (RIP little guy), Alabaster, Dobby, and Haku, who always bring me joy and remind me there is a world outside my head.

And finally, thanks to my partner, Alison. The most wonderful, funny, sexy, smart, *thoughtful* partner I could ever want. I love you, babe!

About the Author

Leigh Harlen is a queer, non-binary writer who lives and works in Seattle with their partner, a very goofy dog named Anya, and a mischief of rats. Their short fiction has appeared in several magazines and anthologies including Pseudopod, Lost Films, and Shoreline of Infinity. Their non-writing hobbies include petting strangers' dogs and enthusing about bats. Find them online at www.leighharlen.com or follow them on Twitter @LeighHarlen.

About the Press

Neon Hemlock is an emerging purveyor of queer chapbooks and speculative fiction. Learn more at www.neonhemlock.com and on Twitter at @neonhemlock.